A Pinch of Time

T0159786

A Pinch of Time

Claude Tatilon

Translated by

Jacob Homel and David Homel

Exile Editions

Publishers of singular
Fiction, Poetry, Drama, Translation, and Nonfiction

2010

Library and Archives Canada Cataloguing in Publication

Tatilon, Claude
    A pinch of time / Claude Tatilon; translated by Jacob Homel and David Homel.

Translation of: La soupe au pistou.
ISBN 978-1-55096-147-8

    I. Homel, David II. Homel, Jacob, 1987- III. Title.

PS8589.A8738S6813 2010   C843'.54   C2010-907140-9

Text © 2010, Le Cherche Midi Editeur
Translation © 2010, Jacob Homel and David Homel
Cover Design by Christine Tatilon
Design and Composition by Digital Structure
Typeset in the Bembo and Didot fonts at Moons of Jupiter Studios
Printed in Canada by Imprimerie Gauvin

The publisher would like to acknowledge the financial assistance of the Canada Council for the Arts and the Ontario Arts Council.

Conseil des Arts du Canada Canada Council for the Arts

ONTARIO ARTS COUNCIL CONSEIL DES ARTS DE L'ONTARIO

This translation was completed with a variety of grants from the Canada Council's National Translation Program for Book Publishing (NTPBP)

Published in Canada by Exile Editions Ltd.
144483 Southgate Road 14 – GD
Holstein, Ontario, N0G 2A0
info@exileeditions.com   www.ExileEditions.com

Canadian Sales Distribution: U.S. Sales Distribution:
McArthur & Company   Independent Publishers Group
c/o Harper Collins   814 North Franklin Street
1995 Markham Road   Chicago, IL 60610
Toronto, ON M1B 5M8   www.ipgbook.com
toll free: 1 800 387 0117   toll free: 1 800 888 4741

For my parents,
newly reunited

Don't ask me what's true and what's not in this story. I'd have to tell you everything's true – down to the last made-up detail.

A word about *pistou*…

For North American gourmets, it might be tempting to read "pesto" for "pistou." Not far from the truth, but not quite right either. Yes, fresh basil is involved, plenty of it, but *pistou* is a soup, not a sauce, something like a minestrone, part French, part Italian.

For gourmets and amateur cooks alike, the recipe can be found at the end of the book. *Bon appétit!*

❧ The Curtain Rises ❧

My first *pistou* lesson was given to me by my mother. I wasn't yet seven and I remember it as if it were yesterday.

We were in Moustiers-Sainte-Marie, one hundred kilometres from Marseille, where I was born. We had just arrived in this charming little village perched in what was known as the Basses-Alpes then, since rechristened Alpes-de-Haute-Provence. When I say we, I mean my mother, my cousin Gérard, and I. This was at the end of June 1943, and my father had been arrested a month before, on the 25th of May, during a secret meeting at the house of the head of the Resistance cell he belonged to. The night the Gestapo arrested him, he was carrying a basil plant and a modest piece of parmesan. The ingredients with which, he would later take pleasure in telling, he had enjoyed, in the Nazi camps, invigorating *pistou* soups that surpassed, or so he claimed, the ones made by my Aunt Virginie. Natzwiller-Struthof, Neue Bremm, Buchenwald, Vaihingen and the last stop, Dachau, where on April 29, 1945, he was freed by the American army. Dad had travelled more than most in his early thirties. When he returned, something no one expected anymore, those orgies of *pistou* hadn't fattened him up: he weighed thirty-six kilos and a whisker!

★

In my family, *pistou* was a sort of tradition. Actually, more like a competition in which my mother and one of her three sisters, Virginie, had long battled for supremacy. The two other sisters had their own specialties: Marie's, the oldest, was fish – *bourride, bouillabaisse,* bass, grilled bream, and flambés with pastis. Henriette's specialty was desserts, and particularly her famous *oreillettes*, or little ears.

Despite my mother's efforts, when it came to *pistou,* Aunt Virginie was the uncontested champ of the family's culinary battles. Today, I still use her recipe. The one I learned on Sundays on the large cast-iron stove, under the attentive supervision of her gourmand husband, Uncle Eugène. Today, I am about to make one for some of my Toronto friends who can't get enough of it.

I lay in front of me the necessary ingredients, bought yesterday with Nela at the St. Lawrence Market. At the center – for we must give credit where credit is due – is basil. *Pistou* for us Provençals. It offers a full bushy head and stands some forty centimetres high. Its strong aroma – close to thyme - makes my mouth water. Here in Toronto, we're lucky: the local basil, grown by the region's Italian farmers and sold under the name *pesto,* competes in nobility and taste with the best Provençal product.

Before me, I have the dog-eared notebook in which I keep my favourite recipes. Aunt Viriginie's occupies the first two pages. It's interesting that although I know these pages by heart, I'd never dare begin a *pistou* operation without first carefully reading them.

★

But let's return to my first lesson on that morning of June 1943. We were on Uncle Émile's terrace – he, the husband of Aunt Marie. They would spend their summers in Moustiers, away from the big city. At the time, the hundred kilometres or so that separated the small village from Marseille were quite a distance, especially by bus. Uncle Émile did have a car, a 1943 front-wheel-drive Citroën that the German army hadn't commandeered, but there was no gas to be found.

The house was empty in early June when we had to flee Marseille to avoid the Gestapo's possible reprisals. My mother, anxious, wanted to think it through, and put off our departure. "I'd be alone with the little one, and so far from Marseille… And what if Paul manages to escape, like Mister Moretti…" But Grandma Rose had taken up her role as the inflexible *mater familias.* Backed up by the rest of the family, ignoring her younger daughter's hesitations, she'd decided for her. "This is serious business and we must hurry, Mireille. You'll leave tomorrow. Gérard will go with you. You'll put them both in school up there." Uncle Émile made the trip with us to open up the house and show us around.

Standing at the top of the village, on a steep slope, the modest house was built over a stable. Its entrance, on one end of a large terrace, overlooked a small garden where a century-old linden tree stood guard. The tree had imposing branches, under whose protection we would while away the hours – clocks run slower in Provence, especially in summer – from breakfast, when the sun was already high in the sky, to supper, when it would disappear behind the mountain. A steep mountain over the village, cut in two in the middle, with its two sides linked by a chain on which was suspended, two hundred and fifty metres above the village, a golden star.

The heavy stone house had been built in the 1880s by Uncle Émile's father, a mason by trade. Later, another floor had been added with three rooms that were reached via an outside staircase on the north side, toward the mountain. There was a *cafoutche* under the staircase, a storage space with old tools and miscellaneous things. A fascinating place for children – almost as much as the stable, which was forbidden to us, though Gérard quickly found the key.

We didn't live in the topmost rooms, too cramped and cut off from the heart of the house for our taste. We slept downstairs, in the rooms that were the extension of the kitchen and that gave onto the village. The smaller room was my mother's, while Gérard and I slept in the larger one with two beds.

During the day, we often climbed upstairs to play. Over Moustiers' mossy rooftops, we'd let our eyes wander across the plain to the blue-hued hills, behind which were hidden Riez-la-Romaine and the Valensole plateau.

One morning – I'll never forget it – we followed a strange aerial ballet for several minutes. Two graceful airplanes twisted and turned in the air, playing out a dance on the vast stage of the sky.

One reached up, then the other descended. They criss-crossed, brushed against each other, hurling wreaths of shooting stars. A slow-motion pas de deux, the slowness explained by the distance of the duel, ten kilometres away. Look at the one on the left! He spiraled up above the other, and made a vertical drop on him. Spirals, tailspins, looping. And always, in slow motion, a myriad of shooting stars. We could barely hear the staggered, dull crackling that gave us an impression of unreal silence. Finally, be it the clumsiness of the gunners or the skill of the pilots, with no salvos hitting the other, eastbound, westbound, the planes divorced for fear of running out of petrol.

An Englishman and an Italian, if we were to believe the opinion of the villagers who had no idea how the aerial hunt ended. Many years later, I like to imagine that one of the planes was French, piloted by Saint-Exupéry on a reconnaissance mission.

The *pistou* is ready.

That name, its two syllables giving rhythm to the nostalgic song of the past, was just a simple meal to devour back then.

Given the circumstances, a very humble dish. No matter; it was enough.

Soon, with the war over, my mother would be able to improve her recipe for the duels when better times returned, when, *pécaïre!*, she'd have to brave her eternal rival, Virginie. It was a time of almost perfect happiness that I would soon come to know. Despite the deep scars, the family would resume its old habits. Under Grandma Rose's veranda, the frame bare, having lost all its window glass during the battle to liberate Marseille, but still offering an impressive view of the Vieux-Port, the harbour, and the islands of Château d'If and Frioul, we would extend the Sunday afternoon suppers – the adults with their endless discussions (why are they making so much noise?), the children with card games or ludo – until the sun would start its descent, which meant the men (Gérard and I first!) could play a few games of *pétanque* in Uncle Eugène's yard, not far away.

"Nicou, would you mind cleaning the terrace table? Hey, not so fast, you missed a spot."

In the meantime, Gérard returned from the Clérissy well in the centre of the village, dragging a heavy watering can from which we would drink, the water cold enough to break your teeth. My mother brought the smoking tureen.

"Bless this humble meal, Lord, which we are about to receive. Gérard, sit up! And get your hair out of your eyes, you look like Madame Sylvestre's cocker spaniel!"

A second serving, more modest than the first: we had to leave some for the evening meal. In these frugal times, appetite didn't exist, only want. Children didn't turn up their noses at soup; they asked for more whenever they could. A fig, cooled in water from the fountain, a drop of honey on a piece of bread, and the meal was over. My mother, after three or four spoonfuls of *pistou*, would finish her meal with linden tea, the best remedy for stomach cramps caused by hunger.

Poverty? Not exactly. We asked for little and greedily took all that was offered. A simple salad? *Amen!* A few blackberries and four almonds? *Panis angelicus!* And freezing-cold water, drunk in great gulps on a linden-scented terrace.

In Moustiers, at the stroke of noon, the heat became unbearable. The great tree was haloed with soft golden light and its diaphanous shadow offered only relative relief. I slowly yielded to its pacifying perfume. After all, it was Gérard's turn to do the dishes today. The torpor of the Provençal summer. From the straw-bottomed upright chair to the chaise lounge was only a step, and quickly taken. I made myself comfortable, ready to listen to the cicadas' concert, for they were already working their wing sheaths above me. A linden flower, an expert glider, was executing a curious spiral descent. My body slowed and sleep took care of the rest, even shooing the flies that never tired of proving their affection for me.

★

"Hey, cooks! Have you fallen asleep?" Nela is at the piano, playing extended arpeggios…

"No, I'm waiting for the water to boil."

She knows the story by heart. I join in the key of F, and loudly sing Uncle Eugène's song:

> *The* pistou *is almost ready,*
> *Almost ready, almost ready.*
> *The* pistou *is almost ready*
> *My dear friend.*
>
> *The veggies and the ham,*
> *How d'you cook 'em, how d'you cook 'em?*
> *Do you boil 'em harder still?*
> *My dear friend.*
>
> *The veggies and the noodles,*
> *Boil 'em hard, boil 'em hard.*
> *But keep the ham away, I say!*
> *My dear friend!*

"But, Uncle, the noodles are going to stick!"

"You're not making Florentine tortiglioni or Bolognese spaghetti, young man! You're making a Provençal *pistou, tron dé pas Diou!*"

"And the San Daniele?"

"Ah, for the ham, you have to wait."

"Isn't San Daniele Italian?"

"Not for long, it'll soon be pro-ven-çal-ized. You'll put it in the soup later. Ask your aunt."

"It's true, *Gàrri*, at the last second, just to warm it up."

"Why?"

"Ask your uncle, the ham is his idea."

"Why… why…? Why do you buy cured ham if you're going to cook it? What are you talking about, Nephew?"

"You're right. It does seem logical."

"Logical! Of course! But that's not the real reason. It's not a cerebral reason – you intellectuals do everything with your noggin! It's a palatal reason! Let me explain…"

"*Boudiou!* You're going to make yourself thirsty, Eugène, with all those big words!"

"True enough, my pretty one. Why don't you bring out the pastis? But don't grab the wrong bottle! The Ricard, not the Pernod that your flighty Félix gave me. He must've thought his father was Parisian… Let me explain, young man: once you take a bite, the unctuousness of the softened pasta will conspire with the velvet of the *pistou* butter. And what will that produce?"

"A… satiny sensation?"

"Good! Satiny! You found it!"

"What else? You've been serving the same sauce for twenty years."

"*Daïse!* Don't exaggerate… A satiny sensation that will excite the more aggressive taste of the pieces of warmed Parmesan. Warmed, not boiled! That's the real reason. *Comprenes, pitchoun?* Come closer: listen to the water hiss, look how it trembles. And those tiny bubbles, do you see them, the bubbles that are jostling to get to the top, under the wide eyes of the oil? Wait, not yet, boy! Wait for the first bubbles... You see, now. Throw in the noodles and the vegetables. And reserve the Parmesan."

↢ ONE ↣

"Are you going to help me, Nela? I'm with the basil."

She interrupts her piano exercises.

"Here I am, my Lord. I shall comb Your head of basil, I shall pluck Your leaves, a little, a lot, passionately… and I shall peel Your six cloves of garlic and will crush them for You. And now I shall grate Your two pieces of cheese: the Parmesan, so white, the red edam, so dry."

"Thank you. Everything is ready for the mixture. Give me the oil."

"Which one?"

"Which one? The olive oil, of course!"

"Here it is: Moulin Saint-Jacques, from the valley of Baux-de-Provence, AOC, extra-Holy Virgin Mary, cold pressed…"

She could have added *fruity, soft, with a scent of fresh almonds.*

A drop on the tip of the finger, the finger on the tip of the tongue.

"It's perfect! Well, maybe a bit more."

"Thank you, Nela, you can go back to the piano."

"And you, Chef, to the stove. When will it be ready?"

"Twenty minutes, maybe. It's barely ten o'clock, don't worry."

"I'm not worried, but you should be. You always say that *pistou* is better heated up and that you have to let it sit for at least half a day before serving."

"I'm right on schedule."

Once, my Aunt Virginie tried to use a blender, given to her by I don't know who. "Never again! All those modern things that turn too fast, I tell you! *Vé*, all it does is make your *pistou* dizzy!" And Uncle Eugène agreed, and went on to damn "blenders, electric whisks and other mixers, nothing but insensitive robots, executing their tasks me-cha-ni-cal-ly… a mortar, a pestle made of olive wood, nothing else! They speak the same language as the garlic, the oil and the basil, they're friends, partners, and that adds a dash of magic. No, never again! A *pistou* made by hand, gently, with the tools of the land." Always a poet, my uncle.

In Toronto, I have my own tools, bought in Aubagne a long time ago. The pestle turns in the mortar, stirring the basil along with memories, some of them terrible.

★

In those dark days, despite the tense atmosphere even a child could feel, I still knew nothing of evil and death. Gérard's unclear and often impatient explanations that tried to trans-

late the sad news around us never really helped me understand.

"Yesterday, the Krauts took Riez."

"Who are the Krauts?"

"Are you dumb or something, Dodo?"

After all, all the members of our family were still quite alive
– Grandma Rose, the oldest, and also Aunt Marie, her oldest
daughter who'd be the first to join her father, Grandpa Félix,
whom I knew nothing about except that he'd often given me
a ride on his knees, if I was to believe an old picture and my
mother's moving memories. And then Dad, the only one
who wasn't there, but he'd gone on a trip, right?

Death made its entrance in my life during our first autumn
in Moustiers, one "fine" morning in 1943 – I would soon turn
seven. An official letter was handed to my mother by a
white-gloved policeman. A letter that said that my father had
succumbed somewhere in Germany during a "train transfer."
As she spoke to me of Heaven, of pink clouds and white
angels, though I didn't understand a word of it, my mother
slipped the fateful letter into her bedroom dresser, between
two sheets that smelled of lavender and that were probably too
small to serve as handkerchiefs, for at night, through the wall,
we could hear her softly weeping.

My young innocence had suffered its first wound.

My first metaphysical questions date from a year and a half
later. On that day, on the platform of the Saint-Charles train
station, I saw my father's walking skeleton come toward me

and bend down to pick me up. A huge smile lit up the bottom half of his face and his teeth seemed awfully impressive. At that moment, I must have understood that our species had received a reprieve.

All in all, my Popaul (that's how I called him later, when I was an adult, in our closest moments) had been lucky. Of the whole family, he was the only one, up until now, to have returned from the afterlife – for a second life that lasted forty years. As for Gérard, I've been waiting ten years for him to come back.

★

Last night, before going to sleep, I reread several of Lafontaine's fables, including "The Young Widow." Despite the profound admiration I've always felt for these wonderful texts full of telling remarks about human nature and illuminated by poetry (my admiration goes back to my first days in school, in Moustiers), I've never been able to read this particular fable without thinking of my mother, and with a serious and grudging reticence about the misogynous comments that show their teeth throughout.

> *A husband's death brings always sighs;*
> *The widow sobs, sheds tears – then dries.*
> *Of Time the sadness borrows wings;*
> *And Time returning pleasure brings.*

A few things bother me straight away. *Sighs*: a word without sufficient strength today. *The widow sobs, sheds tears*: my mother rarely asked for pity through her sobs, and allowed herself to feel grief only away from our eyes. *Then dries*: too quickly this is said, too casually. *Borrows wings*: hmm… this verse is much too beautiful – too sublime – to be criticized. *Pleasure*: pleasure does not return without its share of pain.

A first difference between my mother and this young widow, both of them in their prime, wasn't that my mother never really was a widow – in her heart and her mind she was one, completely – but that her husband, my Popaul, was *handsome, charming, young*, like in that photo from his days in the Navy when, under the tassel, his glowing smile has the exact proportions of the golden mean.

Besides, to say that *And time returning pleasure brings* and that *The frolic band of loves / Came flocking back like doves. / Jokes, laughter, and the dance* would be a striking lie for my mother. For her, there was no triumph of levity and concupiscence, but the triumph of Life through Love. She honestly loved, I've never doubted it, this man ten years her senior (yet still young, barely forty years old) who timidly came knocking on her door, hat in hand, to tell her of days to come and modestly flirt with her, offering a bouquet of wildflowers. Who was able to make her see, through her tears, the buds in the bramble, and convince her that, in their time, flowers would grow again. He accompanied her patiently, hand in hand, on the climbing, broken, uneasy path of rediscovery of her emotional life – there was no shame in being happy. Dear Uncle Roger.

The last lines of "The Young Widow" seem to ring true:

> *And thus, by night and morn,*
> *She plunged, to tell the truth,*
> *Deep in the fount of youth.*

She plunged: voluntarily, with tenacity. Because we must survive.

And my Popaul, on his end, did the same – but in war, without flirtation. With determination. Holding fast. In humid quarries and locked train cars. Never letting go, resisting. Sometimes in minus thirty, in the four rotten corners of the kingdom of Germany.

❧ TWO ❦

Nela pokes her head in the kitchen, inspects the situation at a glance and, reassured by the approximate order that reigns therein, compliments me on the good smell that fills the room. Pure consideration on her part: when a good *pistou* is boiling, there's no need to put your nose near the pot to smell it. She sits down by me and helps by breaking the peapods in two to remove any strings. My soup will be perfect, or it will not be. I feel Eugène looking over my shoulder: it will be perfect!

"Almost done!"

"Do you have a wine in mind for tonight?"

"Yes, a Bandol."

"Have you tasted it?"

"This morning, before putting it in the fridge. The first taste was nothing special."

"A Bandol. At least it'll be in the same palette."

"I hope so. It was expensive enough – thirty dollars. At that price I have to treat it with respect. Would you like a drop?"

"No, thanks."

"Now that it's cool, it's much better. It makes your taste buds tingle. Look at its nice colour, pink running to brick. Taste it."

"Just a drop, then."

"Floral and fruity! Blackberry, blackcurrant, redcurrant and rosemary, with a touch of lavender. What do you think?"

"You know me and wine..."

"Not too bad at all. Its bouquet is a bit short, and so is the finish, unfortunately."

"Remember we have to go to the Portuguese to buy bread."

"You want to go to Nova Era?"

"Why not? We could leave around noon and get a bite to eat there. I could buy some dough for the *filhós* while we're at it. When we get back around three, we'll finish the preparations."

"All right, around noon, then. And the bite seems like a good idea – *uma bifana, um pastel de nata e um galão.*"

"Dominique, make sure the soup has cooled before you put it in the fridge."

★

Dominique, Nicou, Nico, Dodo, Coco... Ah, the story of my nicknames!

"Hurry up, *ensuqué*! D'you hear the church bell? Quarter to six and we're still in the scree. Your mother's going to kill us if we're not back by six. I don't want to be punished again because of you!"

Gérard was right about that, but let's not get ahead of ourselves. The unfairness of his reprimand stung me; I opened wide the doors to a legitimate and pressing anger that charged out of me like a bull into an arena.

"Because of me? And who wanted to come here in the first place? Not me! To the scree! To get bitten by snakes!"

Surprised by my vigorous counterattack, Gérard didn't even try to argue.

"*Ô fan, gounflaïré!* Stop sniffling, it slows you down."

This time my cousin went too far. I refused to take another step.

"And now you're sitting down? And crying? That takes the cake. What is it this time?"

"I'm fed up, you're mean to me."

"Mean? Why are you saying that, Dodo?"

"Because you're always giving me mean names."

"Like what?"

"*Tòti, ensuqué* or *pégon*... And *gouflaïré*, what you just said to me."

"That's not mean, silly!"

"Not mean? You said it with your teeth stuck out, like Nicolas' dog."

"Don't exaggerate!"

"At school, you always call me Dodo, so everyone calls me Dodo now. Except Madame Dupuis, she's the only one who calls me Dominique. Dominique is nicer, don't you think?"

"And Dodo isn't nice? My father, my mother, and Félix all call you Dodo. Don't you like it?"

"Yeah, but Aunt Virginie and Uncle Eugène don't say it the same way. And they always say plenty of nice words like *coco, gàrri,* and *bìcou.*"

"And maybe you like it when your mother calls you Dominique."

"Of course not, she calls me that when she yells at me."

"You see!"

Gérard stood before me, a huge grin on his face, an offered hand, and just like that I was back on my feet again, consoled.

That day, he wasted precious time calming me down, promising never to call me bird names again.

"Swear to God and hope to die. Just Dodo or Dominique. Now, get a move on, *longagne!*"

Oops! He covered his mouth with his hand and hunched his shoulders. "It just sort of slipped out…" Then he laughed happily, which swept any hint of maliciousness from my mind. Once again, like during recess and even in the village streets when he would come to my rescue (even if it was Nicolas' dog or big Jauffret looking for trouble), my dear cousin proved he was on my side. To calm my anxieties, he joked all the way home.

The path was endless: a boulder lay across it and forced us into a detour higher up. Sometimes we tripped over rocks and then kicked them down the slope, where they waited for us, setting traps. Sometimes he took me by the hand, other times by the shoulders, but Gérard helped me quickly make my way through the scree. But even at our fastest, it took too long.

"Do you know what time it is?"

It was half past by the time we got back. Worried sick, giving me a "You're going to get it, Dominique," and Gérard a peremptory "Consider yourself warned," my mother rang out the hour. And she rang our bells hard.

❧ THREE ❦

Suspicion had only grown in my family since the night when, less than a week after my father's arrest, a mysterious Mister Moretti had come to see us at our house at 38 Rue Chaix, in the steep Saint-Victor neighbourhood. We were living in a small apartment built above number 36, a detached house where Grandma Rose and Aunt Henriette lived. This strange visitor arrived late, after the curfew had thrown the city into complete darkness. He told us he'd escaped the Gestapo and had been my father's cellmate for several days. Yes, Paul was doing well. But the interrogations were more and more frequent, and more and more violent. "Look here, on my arm, cigarette burns!" They'd been inflicted on him at SS headquarters at 425 Rue Paradis by a torturer known as Max the Pervert. "And here, my eye!" That had been a gift from a Marseille militiaman named Tortora (you can't make up a name like that; it fit him like a boxing glove). But we shouldn't worry, Paul was built tough, he took pain well. Tough indeed, and resistant in both meanings of the word: he'd leave the Marseille Gestapo several weeks later with only two crushed fingers, a leg broken in three or four places, and a busted knee, thanks to the triangular ruler… Injuries that wouldn't help his career in the concentration camp.

I can still picture Moretti. About fifty years old, bilious eyes in a sunken face. A ferrety look about him.

He asked my mother, "Joseph Millet, have you ever heard of him?"

A wily voice, like the fox in the fable.

"No. I don't know anyone by that name."

If my dear mother didn't tell him, it was because she had nothing to hide.

"Are you sure?

"Yes."

"And if by some chance they came searching the house, did Paul leave anything incriminating behind?"

"Nothing. I mean, except for a few Gaullist pamphlets and the fake IDs."

"Ah! Of course, the fake IDs… They were for the Resistance and the Jewish associations, right? You have to get rid of them right away. Where are they?"

"They were all burned."

"Who burned them?"

"My brother-in-law."

"Good. Is he in the Resistance, too?"

"I don't think so."

"And nothing else besides those pamphlets and the IDs?"

"No."

"What do you know about the arms cache your husband was responsible for?"

"Arms? That's the first I've heard of it. Where is it?"

"I don't know. That's the trouble!"

"Why didn't you ask him?"

"I didn't have the time. We weren't alone in the cell... Please, make an effort to remember... Those weapons are important to us. We must continue the fight, whatever the cost."

"I know absolutely nothing."

He stroked my head with his limp hand – it was awful!

"I'll come back the day after tomorrow, in the evening. That is, if I haven't been picked up first."

He wasn't, and he did come back. But he found only Uncle Eugène in the apartment. Of course, he had nothing to tell him, since he was never involved in the Resistance. With a nose like his, Eugène had quickly smelled a rat.

"So you were with my brother-in-law at the Gestapo?"

"Yes, I was Paul's cellmate for three days."

Well, well! He'd just said "Paul." He knew his real name, though he'd been arrested under his Resistance pseudonym, Claude Baccio.

"You knew him before?"

"No, our networks are well separated. Mine is in Fréjus. That's where I was arrested. But tell me, you must know something about the arms cache he was in charge of. As you can imagine, we're cruelly short of everything, weapons, munitions, explosives... It's hard to steal from the Krauts, and London barely supplies us."

How could Moretti have known? Eugène himself knew nothing. My father had never told him about the arms cache, hidden in a mausoleum in the Saint-Pierre cemetery. Only Jo knew: he, and he alone, helped my father receive and distribute the merchandise. Among other feats, in December 1942, the weapons had contributed to an impressive show of fireworks. Three explosions in the Gulf of Lion had deprived Rommel's Afrika Korps of a few hundred men, a few thousand litres of gasoline, and quite a few boxes of ammunition, and at quite an opportune moment too, barely a month after the September 8th Anglo-American landing in North Africa, as the German Field Marshal struggled to keep the advantage in that theatre of operations.

First, my father and Jo had taken the explosives out of the cache and brought them to Bonnet. He, a dock worker and middleman, brought them to the harbour and gave them to Sandre, also a dock worker, but a diver by trade, who attached the explosives to the ship's hull as it was leaving for Libya. Then, once the boat had left Marseille, *boom!*

"Try and remember. It really is important."

"I don't know any more than my sister-in-law."

"Ah. Well. A pity. By the way, where is your sister-in-law?"

"I don't have a clue. She was frightened by her husband's arrest. She left with her son, and I don't have an address for her."

"She didn't even tell her mother?"

"She told no one."

Eugène tried to avoid looking him in the eye to hide what he felt about him.

"We haven't heard anything. And we're very worried."

"Do you know a Millet? A Joseph Millet?"

"No."

Did he ever know how to ask questions! Not the brightest light, for sure. Eugène gave him a failing grade, which didn't stop the traitor from asking more questions.

"What a mess! Their whole network has been dismantled, and we have no way of getting our hands on those weapons, which would really be useful! All their members have been arrested, and…"

"All except one!" Eugène thought, ignoring the conversation.

Jo, known as the *Goï*, who had known Eugène since elementary school, had come to his office the day after the arrests, and my uncle had hidden him in his house for two days. Jo had told him everything he knew about the arrests. How he'd had the good fortune of slipping through the net – a real stroke of luck! A few metres from the home of Gaston C., the doctor whose house was being used for an emergency meeting between six and seven-thirty, Jo thought he'd glimpsed a uniform through the slightly open door and had continued on his way – but still rather slowly, due to the street being so steep and the fact that he limped (which is why he was called *Goï*, meaning "lame" in Provençal – polio at the age of nine). He'd had enough time to think and convince himself that he'd actually seen a uniform. A German uniform.

Reaching the top of the street, he crossed it, came back down the opposite sidewalk, then took a room at the Azur Hôtel, a little farther down. From there, he was able to follow the proceedings. He'd seen Borel followed by Casta at 6:45, then Autran, the last to arrive, at 6:53, walk straight into the trap. A covered truck came at 7:20, and the prisoners filed out: the doctor first, the head of the network, then ten other comrades. The entire network!

The nineteen other members had been picked up in the preceding days. First Armand, on the 17th, as he was leaving his office, with compromising papers on him.

Then Maguy, four days later. Arrested as she got off her bike, on the quay of the transporter bridge, where she was to meet her contact, a man named Mathieu, to whom she'd already given several messages the doctor had entrusted her with. She knew right away that this was no ordinary check of her papers; the SS officer who stopped her asked no questions. He tore the bike from her hands, took the rubber tips off the handlebars and removed the precious piece of rolled paper. She spotted Mathieu making his way toward the bridge. He easily managed to hide in the crowd waiting for the craft to take them to the other side of the Vieux-Port.

Then, that same evening, it was Berthier, the network telegraph operator's turn. He was caught red-handed sending messages. He hadn't seen the unmarked car that had been circling his hideout for the last day.

One after the other, until they got Fred, the young police inspector who, two days earlier, had been caught stealing stamps at the Prefecture office.

Now, Jo was alone.

"Your sister-in-law told me about some maps and pamphlets that were hidden here…"

Eugène jumped back into the conversation before the next question.

"Right. I told her she'd better burn it all. To avoid trouble."

"You did well. Anything else you can tell me?"

You can go straight to hell! But he didn't tell him that. He showed him to the door in a completely civil manner.

No one ever saw Mr. Moretti again. Had he realized he'd been unmasked? Probably not. Unlike Mireille, his young, naïve sister-in-law, Uncle Eugène wasn't born yesterday. In fact, he was quite the actor and had been rehearsing for years with his dear Virginie. Had this strange Mr. Moretti been stabbed without pomp or circumstance on the corner of some dimly lit street by a Resistance fighter, *à l'agachon?* Had the Nazis given him a new mission of treachery? Or had they simply put him behind bars to thank him for his loyal services?

Whatever the situation was, he never bothered us again.

But a few days after this second visit, a policeman, escorted by two German soldiers, came to ask Grandma Rose a few questions about my mother and me. She was posted at her usual spot on the Joseph-Étienne Square, not too far from the Saint-Victor church, where she'd been selling fish for the past two decades. While setting up her day's offerings on a bed of seaweed – red mullet, sardines, gurnard surrounded by a sea of mussels, and to one side, a large piece of tuna, its flesh a dark red, that she would cut into thick slices and sell well before ten in the morning – the escort arrived. She had no trouble understanding, despite the policeman's debonair attitude, that at seven in the morning, this was no friendly visit. And since she often went to the cinema, she'd been able to hide the shudder that ran up and down her spine and to soften up the nice policeman, who did not suffer from excess zeal. She was nothing but a mother, worrying herself sick for her lost children. Where are they? Oh, dear! I would give, sirs, all the fish I own to know. The policeman did not insist, and he walked away with his goose-stepping escort.

But the Gestapo did not stop there. The next day, around seven-thirty in the evening, another escort made its way to Rose and Henriette's, who were about to sit down for supper. This is a search, ladies! Every corner of the house investigated, especially the cellar that was level with the yard.

"And their apartment, upstairs?"

"Empty."

"Do you have the key?"

"Yes."

The little kitchen, the bedroom, the alcove and the bathroom. Empty.

Rose and Henriette were never bothered again.

★

At the time, when it came to food, the country no doubt offered superior resources to the city. Marseille, far from good agricultural land, wasn't supplied very well. There was fish, of course… Except that a third of the local catch was skimmed off by the occupying army, another third sold at top prices to restaurant owners and the rich, and the stallholders had to scramble for what was left – the smallest third – at the morning auction at the Rive-Neuve Quay. Tricks and schemes of all sorts were devised. We called it the "G" system – G for get by or get hungry. It was hard to make your way through the maze of the black market and reel in your line without having it stripped. Rose knew this only too well, for she was able to open her modest, open-air business only three or four mornings a week. And despite all the effort she put into it, considering the difficulty of the times, the plates and bellies of her daughters were never full. Yet she wasn't stingy, keeping for her family, despite the monetary losses, a large part of the fish she'd been able to get through *pòti* (a curious Provençal word meaning "barter"), though it was not always to her advantage: a monkfish tail for half a kilo of artichokes, traded with Eugène and Rachel, her neighbours, who owned a small fruit and vegetable business a few metres from her stall. Or she'd barter with François, the owner of the bar that opened onto the square: two slices of tuna for a measure of sugar. Like most French people, Rose panicked at the idea of running out of sugar. In fact, we ran out of everything. Nothing we ate, in too small quantities, could fill our stomachs.

Which is why, at the end of the summer of 1943, when the danger of being taken by the Marseille Gestapo vanished along with my father, who in July was sent on the painful path to the concentration camps (so Jo the *Goï* had told Uncle Eugène), my mother decided to extend our stay in Moustiers. "When school starts again, the children will attend here."

❧ FOUR ❧

In October of 1943, we found ourselves in Madame Dupuis' one-room schoolhouse. Gérard, 11 years old by then, was in the older boys' division. I would be turning seven in January and was part of the youngest group. My first time in a classroom! About time, too: the Wehrmacht's occupation of the free zone in November 1942 and the far too common sound of air-raid sirens had dissuaded my parents from putting me in school when I turned six.

One-room schools are an excellent solution, if I'm to trust my own experience. By January I could read, having learned – the Berlitz method, the intensive kind – by listening to others. At first there weren't many of us – less than ten, if memory serves me. Three older kids: André Jauffet, Louis Achard, and Gérard. Four in the middle: the Bourjac sisters, Jackie and Anne, Antoine Audibert, the mayor's son, and Dany, our teacher's daughter. Three young ones: the Lemoine kids, Jean and Martine, and I, Dominique (Dodo during recess). The older kids wanted to show the younger ones what they knew, and we, admiringly, took them as models and did everything to impress them. As for the children in the middle group, they lived under the double influence of emulation and domination. A situation that seems to me pedagogically ideal, especially when I compare it to the overloaded classrooms I'd sit in later, in Marseille and Aubagne, where I'd often find myself with more than thirty other children.

Ah, but wait, there were actually eleven of us with Jésus Fernandez! How could I have forgotten him, with his skin much darker than ours – probably from his gypsy or Berber blood, for he came from Córdoba – and his blue eyes? He is at the source of one of my most striking memories.

It was toward the end of the first semester, in November, during a visit by the superintendent. Madame Dupuis had told us not to worry. Everything would be fine, the superintendent was a nice man; we shouldn't feel intimidated and should offer polite and clear answers to his questions.

He certainly was a nice man. And far from intimidating with his slight lisp. "Hello, kidsh… I will ashk a few queshtions and you will anshwer me ash if I were your teacher."

He had a soft voice, and asked his questions with smiles of encouragement.

"What ish your name?"

"Gérard, sir."

"All right, Gérard, how did you sholve the problem?"

Madame Dupuis seemed happy that Gérard had been chosen, while I feared for him. I remember clearly: there were two trains that would meet each other, one leaving Nice, the other

Marseille. And not at the same time, to top it off! We had to figure out the time and place they would meet. And the trains weren't even travelling at the same speed – talk about tough!

"Can show us how you did it?"

"Yes, sir."

He pointed convincingly to the graph Madame Dupuis had drawn for us. "Train A leaves Nice at 7:45 a.m. and is going at 60 kilometres an hour. Between Marseille and Nice, there are 200 kilometres, and the train doesn't make any stops. Train B leaves Marseille at 8:15 a.m. and travels 90 kilometres an hour; it doesn't stop either."

"Very good. And then?"

"By the time Train B leaves the station, Train A has gone… I used the rule of three: 60 times 30 divided by 60. Simplifying, 60 on one side, 60 on the other, that makes 30 kilometres. That means there is a distance between the two trains of 200 minus 30, or 170 kilometres."

"You're on the right track. Continue."

"Now, I express the proportions between the two speeds as fractions, as our teacher showed us."

He wrote on the blackboard: "Speed of A: $^2/_5$; speed of B: $^3/_5$."

"That's good. Now you have to figure out the time and place the trains meet. How will you do that?"

"I use fractions. First, I calculate distance. When the trains meet, Train A will have gone two-fifths of 170 kilometres. I divide by 5 and multiply by 2. That makes 68 kilometres. Add to that the 30 kilometres it travelled before B started. Total distance: 98 kilometres."

"And how far will B have travelled?"

"Well, there are two ways to calculate that. Either you subtract 98 from 200, or I re-calculate with the fraction $^3/_5$. Either way, I get 102 kilometres."

"And by doing both calculations, you're also verifying your sums."

"Yes, sir. I check that my results are correct."

"Continue: the time and place where both trains meet."

"The location is easy. It is 102 kilometres from Marseille and 98 from Nice (98+102 = 200). The time is easy, too: Train A is going 60 an hour so it travels the 98 kilometres in... the rule of three: 98 times 60 divided by 60 makes 98 minutes. So 1 hour and 38 minutes, that I add to its departure time: 7:45 + 1 hour and 38 minutes... 8 and 5 make 13, I put down 3 and carry the 1, 4 and 3 make 7; 7 and 1 make 8... 83 minutes, so 1 hour and 23 minutes. Total: 9:23 a.m. That's when the trains meet."

"Now what do you do?"

"Now I check my results with Train B: 102 minutes times 60 divided by 90. I'll simplify that: multiplied by 2 and divided by 3. So 68 minutes. So 1 hour and 8 minutes. I add to my departure time, which also gives me 9:23 a.m."

"Impresshive, young man!"

We were all impressed. Madame Dupuis was beaming, as much as her daughter and almost as much as me, and much more than Jauffret and Achard. I'm proud to have such a smart cousin. He's proud as a peacock, too. Tomorrow I'll go get the water at the fountain instead of him. If *Maman* lets me.

Things didn't go as well with the vocabulary lesson. I remember it was based on a small text – by Anatole France, I think – that talked about the Tuileries, in Paris, and some sparrows splashing around in a puddle.

"You, *Jesús*."

"Whew! It wasn't me, it was Fernandez! When the superintendent pronounced his name with a Spanish accent, with the *jota* sound, his lisp disappeared.

"Tell us, what is the sparrow doing in the second sentence?"

A long silence and a desperate look.

"Go on, make an effort… Can't you see? Read us the sentence."

Embarrassed by his strong Spanish accent, our classmate complied.

"You know, sir, our little Spanish refugee has only been in France since last spring."

So much tenderness in her voice: "Our little Spanish refugee."

"I see, only six months…"

The superintendent spoke to him in Spanish. Probably to tell him something like, "*Jesús, yo también, quando hablo tu lengua, tengo un acento extranjero muy fuerte.*" He continued in French: for a young boy like him, there would be no problem

46

and that very soon he'd be speaking as well as his classmates. And he was right. Barely six months later, our little refugee could have passed for any one of us, at least on a moonless night.

"Your accent will get better very soon. Just by listening to your classmates. Now, tell us, what does *hop* mean, as in *the sparrow hops?*"

A heavy, stubborn silence.

"Now, you know this. Look at me."

So the superintendent, ruddy, smallish, sixty, and paunchy, began courageously – nothing must halt militant pedagogy – to jump up and down. For a few long seconds.

"*Jesús*, look at me. What am I doing?"

Still no answer. The superintendent kept on trying, stoically, though he seemed in desperate need of dance lessons. Meanwhile, he lavished endless and slightly breathless encouragements on Jesús.

"All right, at least try, son."

So, finally, opening his mouth – does not pedagogical perseverance break down all walls? – our Jesús took a deep breath and dove in, though he wasn't sure he knew how to swim. Hunching his shoulders and casting his distressed blue eyes at his comical inquisitor, he spoke, timidly, but oh so audibly.

"You acting *estupid!*"

It was the right answer.

During recess, Gérard was a hair's breadth from beating him up. "Damn Spaniard, can't you learn to speak French?

You made trouble for Madame Dupuis!" He was a bit of a hothead as a child, my dear cousin, and not too politically correct.

Luckily for Jesús, Jauffret intervened. "Leave him alone, Gé! Or else…" And since he was a head taller than Gérard… Besides, Jesús was the son of the sexton of the very Catholic church of Moustiers-Sainte-Marie. You can imagine, with a name like Jesús…

But things didn't stop there. There was no love lost between Gérard and Jauffret. One day, I imprudently sat in the spot that was exclusively his under the covered part of the playground. Jauffert chased me off with insults and began to run after me, hand in the air, across the playground and even a few times around the tall plane tree that occupied its centre. Gérard came to my rescue: with a well-placed foot, he sent Jauffret flying through the air as the other students laughed and mocked him. But he picked himself up in a flash, with his fists up this time. Gérard stood a few metres away, as stiff as justice. The magisterial sound of the whistle stopped play. Madame Dupuis came and took the petulant boy by the ear and put his nose against the tree that would be his cell until the end of recess.

Knowing his day of glory had arrived, Gérard put on a wide smile, making sure it was seen by Jauffret, who could do nothing but look at him menacingly.

❧ FIVE ❧

My mother had invited him for supper. I was sitting on the terrace when he arrived, playing ludo with Gérard on the ground. I can still see him as he stood before us, tall in the open gate. It's the first image I remember of him.

He was wearing big black shoes, corduroy pants, a dark jacket over a white shirt. His open collar showed off a powerful neck. He stood in the silence, as if leaning against the mountain to his right, pink now with the setting sun. His face, lit by a radiant smile, was as wide as the sky. He was a handsome man, and tall. Yet he didn't wear his encroaching baldness well. He wasn't old – older than *Maman*, sure, but not old. He was strong, Monsieur Roger, and seemed nice.

"Just call me Roger, kids! Roger." On the first day, no less. Uncle Roger, only a few months later.

He did everything to make our stay in the country as comfortable as possible. For example, with Gérard's help, he carried a big metal basin all the way to our house. He'd borrowed the basin from his friend Bertrand, the mechanic, who'd used it for oil changes. He cleaned it up in the little yard below, then set it in one corner of the kitchen, next to the fireplace. It would become our bathtub.

During the lavender harvest, a distillery on the road to Riez, just before the switchbacks that led to the village, would shower Moustiers with its perfume. Two or three times a week, Roger would bring large demijohns filled with lavender water, still hot. And so it was, two or three times a week, we were energetically scrubbed and scoured by strong hands deaf to our protests; my mother didn't joke around when it came to personal hygiene.

My father also had his tubs: the ones that belonged to the Marseille Gestapo on Rue Paradis, then in Paris, on Rue des Saussaies, in which only his head would be immersed. Then the ones in the camps, perfumed with disinfectant, in which he was completely immersed, head and all. The Germans had an awful fear of lice, which could spread typhus.

My Popual also took relatively frequent showers. "The first time I took one," he told me once, "was at Neue Bremm, my first station of the Cross. We were naked in a row in front of the bathhouse. People started to whisper that some of the camps had gas chambers and that they were disguised as showers… You can imagine the reaction! The Krauts had to push us in with the butt of their guns. Once we got inside, under the showerhead – would it be water or gas? – we were panicking like sheep at the slaughterhouse! So Caraco, in a funereal voice, starts in: 'Brothers, now is the time to recommend your soul to God and say your prayers! And if I were you, I'd do it on the double!' His sense of humour gave us courage and we started laughing – even those who didn't speak a word of French. He actually started praying for real. His prayer was answered, and we were saved."

In the evening, when the mountain disappeared and the horizon started to fade, the time came for us to leave the terrace and go into the kitchen, already in shadow. *Maman* would make her way through the dark room and pick up the large box of matches she left on the mantelpiece. Then she went to the white porcelain oil lamp that a complicated weight and counterweight system kept hanging from the ceiling, above the table. She lifted the glass tube, cracked a match and touched the wick: the kitchen would light up. It was a large square room with sooty walls, the patina of years of flames from the fireplace at the far wall. In all seasons, an indescribable scent hovered in the room – burnt wood, old things. That smell will remain in my nose and my mind, even if I live to be a hundred. Just like childhood memories.

We sat around the large table in the centre of the room. The table was covered by a yellow oilcloth with small red and blue flowers, faded in places from having been scrubbed too often. To the left of the door, the stone *pile* and its copper tap. "Nicou, turn off the tap all the way, please, that dripping will drive me mad!" Next to it, the water pump. "Go on, Gérard, work those biceps!" On the far side, facing the door, a large buffet built into the wall, much too large for the meagre food inside. To its left, the imposing fireplace and its mantelpiece, on which stood a series of yellowing photos displaying the generations of Uncle Émile's family. There, the third from the right, our dear uncle, whom Gérard noticed straight away because of his harbour fireman's uniform. In another picture, a whiskered married man on his bicycle and his timid wife, surrounded by a crowd of family members squeezed one against the other. My favourite: Émile's father. His moustache is slightly smaller, he's wearing hunting clothes, his cartridges around his waist, his game-sack slung over his shoulder (from which a rabbit or a hare's ears seemed to be sticking out), rifle at his feet. Next to the pictures, another oil lamp, a portable one, and the big box of matches.

Whoever saw us there, preparing a game of cards or ludo in the yellowish light of the lamp, would think he was gazing upon an allegory of happiness. Yet in less than an hour, my mother would begin her nocturnal weeping again.

"She's crying less these days," the all-seeing Gérard would point out. In fact, when you watched her carefully, you saw she was slowly changing – a bit less sad, a bit less grey, less on edge. Roger was, of course, not incidental to this miraculous metamorphosis.

And the next spring, this observation: "Your mother's lighter now, Dodo. Her heart isn't as heavy." A regular soap bubble.

My cousin's remark struck my imagination. With a child's eyes, I saw my mother's heart turn into a red balloon and, filled with the helium of love, carry her off, gaily laughing, a metre above the ground. When my turn came to experience the big thrill, each time I would hear my cousin tell me, "You've gotten lighter." A time would come when the image of a hot-air balloon would take over from the simple red balloon. I had grown up, and my horizons expanded.

❧ SIX ❧

With Roger's help, the *cafoutche* was turned into a henhouse. We had two hens now, a white one and a red one, and they took turns laying an egg every other day. Gérard quickly adopted the red one. He would sit on the ground and call, "Hey, Ginger!" She would flutter over to him and perch on his shoulder to receive her reward: a snail or a fat worm that was wriggling around her benefactor's finger. Three or four eggs a week – not bad at all.

"Kids, Roger is turning forty today. He's going to have supper with us. Cousin Jeanne agreed to give me a head of basil and a bunch of vegetables from her garden, so I made a *pistou*."

"Great, *Maman*!"

"And Jules the butcher gave me a nice piece of pork rind. But there are still a few hairs on it."

"Don't worry, Auntie, we'll shave it."

"With shaving cream?"

"Of course not, *fadòli!* Your mother will boil it first, then we'll use her tweezers. You'll see, it's easy."

"Have you ever done it before?"

"No, but I know how."

"And for dessert, I'll make you some eggnog!"

"I know about eggs, but what are nogs?"

"What is it, Auntie?"

"You'll see. It's delicious and very good for you."

A litre of milk from Noiraude, Norine's black goat that spends her days grazing in front of our terrace and talks to us when we play near her, two egg yokes, a pinch of saccharine and a spoonful of orange-blossom water. You beat it until it froths...

"Auntie, are brown eggs better than white ones?"

Ah! Gérard and his questions...

"Your eggnog's delicious, my little chick!" Uncle Roger told *Maman*, his face red as a flame. He got up, his napkin still around his neck, drinking down a second big gulp. "Now just a minute..."

Our connoisseur Roger opened the cupboard door.

"I'm going to 'disinfect' it with some hooch. There's a bit left. One drop will do, and your brother-in-law won't smell what's missing."

"My godfather's a harbour fireman. He can smell things from far away."

Birthday or not, Gérard, who had great affection for his godfather, was ready to defend him.

"That's just an expression, my boy! Your godfather and I have been friends forever. You know he's my *pétanque* partner."

"He's even the team captain!"

"You're right. He's the captain because he's the shooter."

"Yes, but, Gérard, the pointer is also an important player! He's the one who scores the points."

"Not always."

Gérard could be pretty annoying. He always had to be right. I knew he liked Roger, but he liked Uncle Émile even more. I could understand: we'd known him for much longer. Still, he wasn't as much fun as Roger.

"Can I have a little more, please, *Maman*?"

"There's none left, dear."

No cake, no candles – no matter: the dessert, filled with "Happy Birthday!" and "Best Wishes!" was a great success. Such a success that *Maman* promised to make her eggnog every Sunday, for breakfast. We would enjoy it on the terrace or in the kitchen depending on the season, in our favourite chairs, our legs stretched out. "Gérard, don't lick your chops like that, it isn't polite!" I can't remember a single time when my mother broke her delicious tradition. But she would never drink any of the magic beverage herself.

"Much too fattening for me."

★

Sunday afternoon. The square in front of the church was as full as an egg and loud as a henhouse, with peeps, clucks and cock-a-doodle-dos… At the centre of the crowd, Uncle Émile and

Roger, in full concentration. In the front row, Gérard and I, excited beyond measure. That's it! They've made the finals. They've just stolen their fourth victory – 15 to 13 – against Clément the mailman, a truly elite shooter, and his partner, an excellent pointer from Riez whose name I've forgotten.

Their first match was a breeze. They played – luckily enough – against Tavé and Marcel. A redoubtable double, but only for the spectators: they run on rosé and when they shoot, watch your legs! At ten o'clock, by the time the tournament started, they had already reached their usual state.

The other matches were much harder. The fourth, which lasted from three to four-thirty, should have been televised, had television existed at the time.

And now, the grand finale against a double from Puymoisson who, in four matches, had already forced two teams to *baiser Fanny*.[1] The Puymoisson double was a real power-house: they *estanquent* their balls full throttle and sent them to kiss the jack in the *gàrri* two times out of three! Émile and Roger were going to lose, but we didn't know that yet, of course. And since they were leading in points at the beginning of the game, we were happy as can be. "Don't make so much noise, kids! Wait, Roger! Let me get this *gratton* out of your way, it's right in your alley."

I could practically tell the story of this match, ball by ball, up until the fifteenth and final point, without inventing a single play – or almost. Which shows that, when sown in fertile soil, childhood memories leave indelible traces. But I'll just describe the key moments. After 10 to 8, then 11 to 8, then 12 to 8 for our team, suddenly it was 12 to 11! Émile, the shooter, just missed two balls. Too much emotion, no doubt. Their adversaries got the jack back, but sent it at least nine metres away, maybe more (what about the rules?), to a spot covered with gravel (ah, how sneaky they are!). Their first ball wasn't their best, but Roger couldn't take advantage. He was nervous and wasted his own shot. He squatted, furious, feet perfectly *tanqués* in the circle, knees apart, and pointed the second. The ball had barely left his fingers when he got up in a flash and followed it all the way to the jack. "Come on, *maï*, my pretty thing! Just a bit…" It came close, no doubt, but it wasn't that good of a shot either – a smidgen too short and not really in the right spot. The proof? Bang, 12 to 12! And then, ouch, 12 to 13. Émile, with a hard shot, kicked the right *botche* away, but a bad bounce also pushed Roger's, which was holding the point. Yes or no? No or yes? Yes! 13 to 13. They won't go down easily, the home team. Everything is possible.

Then came the moment of truth. Émile was playing the decisive ball, the last one of the game. Destiny lay between his hands. If he shoots the opponents' ball (without a bad bounce), the game is in the bag, and they win the big sack of potatoes that goes to the winning team. If he misses, see you later, 'taters: the trophy and the glory go to the other team.

The ball twitched slightly in his hand. He swung his body back and forth, knees lightly bent, his left arm rocking to ensure stability. The ball was raised to nose level, his left eye closed to perfect his aim, Émile was about to…

All around, eyes stared, mouths opened in painful grimaces, hearts and lungs skipped a beat.

Oh! The ball arched in a hard shot.

A dull noise: a hole, and that's it! A good twenty centimetres from theirs, mockingly illuminated by a teasing sunbeam.

> *A pétanque game,*
> *It's always fun*
> *Don't you cause shame*
> *By hitting the wrong one*
> *You aim and miss*
> *You change your shot*
> *The ball and its hiss*
> *As the battle is fought.*

❧ SEVEN ❧

Roger turned a section of the small yard facing the *cafoutche*, a metre and a half above the terrace, into a vegetable garden. We were still waiting for the first results, but we wouldn't wait for long. Soon we'd be picking the most delicious tomatoes I've ever eaten in my life.

Uncle Roger – that's how Gérard and I called him since… well, since he started kissing my mother on the lips – helped us in so many ways. From time to time he brought us poor little birds taken warm, straight from the traps he set at the foot of the olive trees. Gérard and I participated actively in the great hunt by providing him the *aludes* with which he baited his traps. These harmless winged ants swarmed around the linden tree and were easier to catch than flies. Roger promised that one day he would bring us with him into the hills and give us a lesson on how to set traps.

Then there were the snails we harvested after every storm. In Moustiers, a storm is a sight to see! The sky literally crashes down on your head. The rolling thunder orchestrates it all, its directions amplified by the resonance of the mountains, and it trumpets the arrival of curtains of rain – when it's not hail – that drum down on everything in a deafening crash.

Suddenly, a thick fog makes half the terrace disappear, and strong gusts of wind whip the linden's mop of hair. Terrified, we would hide in the kitchen, lights off, doors and windows shut tight, squeezed together as if in King Kong's fist. My mother, who trembled as much as we two boys did, could not find a single comforting word.

Then, abruptly, it all stops, leaving a dizzying silence. Then come the cries of the crows cawing from their shelters. We open the door: the fog is lifting, the sky straightening itself. Little by little the terrace recovers its proper size, and the linden tree is calm. When we were sure the storm had travelled far enough – on to Verdon or Valensole – we ventured outside, relieved and reassured, as if waking after a long sickness. "Don't forget your little bag for the snails!" The rainwater, having accumulated on the Vénascle plateau, the mountain's buttress, hurtled down into the enormous funnel above the village. What a show!

Our friend the linden tree shook itself off as we passed. Around us, nature slowly raised her head again. Exalted by the rain, even the smallest blade of grass – of thyme, of mauve, of *pèbre d'aï* – sent out its scent in the still shimmering air. And Gérard, euphoric, declared, "To the gastropods!" His straight-A erudition from the older group never ceased to amaze me.

We took the Riou Road that went right in front of the house, on the large sloping field covered with bramble and weeds: Noiraude's territory. She was always a little fearful after a storm and slow to come out. We caught our best prey on fennel stalks: Burgundies and small greys by the dozen. Gérard kept the tiny ones for his hens.

Back home, we set our loot in the wire-netted crate that Uncle Roger built for us. He called it the *sapès,* the snails' dieting room. After the customary eight days of snail fasting, *Maman* made us a feast in her style: snails *à la suçarelle!* A tomato, two garlic cloves, fennel, and a dribble of olive oil. "A real pleasure!" Gérard, worthy son of Eugène, invariably declared, putting on a show by sucking his fingers and smacking his lips. Once, I remember, sated, full to the brim, he refused his aunt's tempting offer of another small grey with a great, "No, thank you, Auntie! The others are still crawling in my stomach!"

Olive oil was measured by the drop. In those difficult times, there was an almost complete absence of fats and, to make them even more virtual, rationing cards were rationed too. But Uncle Émile, who owned a few dozen olive trees around Moustiers, sold his produce to the Riez cooperative, which paid him in heavy, glistening coins. He shared his wealth with us once or twice a year: a bottle filled with liquid gold. Beautiful brownish-gold tempered with hints of green that my mother, aware of its worth, would use only for special meals, being careful, of course, not to waste a single drop.

★

Last month, *Maman* found herself a paying job. Overnight, she became an artist for her brother-in-law Émile's nephew who owned a small family company in Marseille that made "luminary art" – which meant he designed and manufactured, with the help of his wife and son, lampshades for certain department stores, like the Dames de France. Every week, the bus from Marseille dropped off a few hundred lampshades, unmounted and cut from Celluloid or oiled paper. With her tongue stuck out and her brows furrowed, she had to colour the drawings traced on the shades: Provençal landscapes and Nativity figures. She worked from daybreak to dusk, but at least she received a few pennies for her work, and they were added to what Grandma Rose and Uncle Eugène would send her.

On the day this commercial enterprise began, Gérard decided to make a painting of our beautiful village, and propose it for use on a shade. He couldn't stop talking about it.

Finally he finished it. With the two mountain peaks in the background, linked by the chain, his work was fairly good, though *Maman* thought the yellow star that hung from the chain in the middle of the drawing was out of proportion. I liked it the way it was.

Through the years, and many changes of address, I miraculously held on to a copy of this expressionist landscape. I have to admit, with its large star that changes reality, it still speaks to me. And with everything it reminds me of, I wouldn't trade it for anything other than a Cézanne.

Urged on by Uncle Roger, whose charm would always conquer *Maman*'s reluctance, I managed to persuade her to send Gérard's work to Marseille. What's the worst that can happen, Mireille? It fell into the hands of Monsieur Lacroix, the head of the lighting department at Dames de France, and supposedly everyone loved it. Monsieur Lacroix immediately ordered several dozen copies.

The gentleman's real name was Rosenberg. Not too long after this unexpected order, his flowery name – most probably divulged by a well-intentioned neighbour – would earn him a one-way ticket to Auschwitz.

My cousin was grateful for my help in turning him into a landscape painter and, to thank me, he let me smoke one of his cigarettes, made from carefully chosen stems (they had to be the right size, their holes wide enough to let the smoke go through) that he hid in the stable. It was an impressive scene, and I still remember its emotional charge: our clandestine entry into a forbidden place, the disquieting protests of the rusty lock, the sweet scent of mould and dust, the dark recesses that our wavering candle couldn't quite illuminate. And then, in a solemn ceremony, from a dark corner Gérard would produce a large pack of cigarettes, held tightly by an elastic like the sticks Madame Dupuis would give us for calculus lessons.

The cigarette between his thumb and forefinger, like Uncle with his fat yellow *gitanes,* Gé gave a great big pull on the cigarette to light it from the candle flame – what imprudence in a place full of dry wood! As for me, nothing, not a memory. I've forgotten everything about my smoke. Did the pathetic contraband cigarette make me cough? Did I smoke it to the end? Not a memory, even of its taste. It surely had the delicious scent of transgression – a repressed memory, people nowadays would say.

❧ EIGHT ❧

Uncle Roger was a truck driver. At least he became one after he had to leave Toulon, where he worked as a mechanic. Last year he came to Moustiers to live with his sister and brother-in-law, in the latter's family house, to avoid his Compulsory Work Service. Roger was from Toulon, but his sister, twelve years his senior, had married a dyed-in-the-wool Mousterian, which explained why he knew Moustiers like the back of his hand, and was considered a true son of the soil.

"Didn't feel like working for the Krauts!"

He wouldn't have been sent to Germany straight away, since at its inception in February 1943, the CWS[2] recruited only from young people born in 1920, 1921, and 1922. But Roger feared the situation would get worse, and he was right. Less than a year later, the demands of the occupiers increased, and the Vichy government was forced to extend the CWS "to all women without children, aged between 18 and 45, and all men between 16 and 60 years of age." At the end of March 1943, Roger closed his garage – where he'd been twiddling his thumbs anyway since the truce of June 22, 1940 – and left everything behind. Everything but the Berliet truck that he drove to Moustiers. His "old friend from the thirties," which now ran on a gasifier, would help him start his own transportation business: scrap metal, fruits and vegetables, lavender and, more often than not, manure for the market gardens.

Due to "that providential excrement that doesn't exactly fall from the sky," he assured us we'd soon have the "best *pommes d'amour* in the country." That's what we called tomatoes in our part of the world. He installed the gasifier on the Berliet all by himself. Mechanic – that was his true calling. He even had a diploma from the Aix-en-Provence vocational school. *Maman* was right when she said, with a hungry look I didn't quite understand, that Roger could do anything with his hands. I was much more impressed by his biceps. When they flexed, they almost burst through his shirt sleeves.

Does anyone know what a gasifier is these days? A large metallic cylinder set vertically at the back of the vehicle's cabin in which charcoal was burned. The combustion created poor quality gas – a mix of carbon, hydrogen, and nitrogen, if I correctly remember Roger's explanations – with a low energy value.

Before starting the vehicle, Roger had to wait for the gases to build up in the cylinder; usually it took a good quarter of an hour. Then it was "Whip it, coachman!" Sometimes he had to languish, as he put it, on the roads he travelled, since the smallest slope would force him to downshift into first. "But the countryside is so pretty around here! It would really be a shame to rush through it."

No risk of that, Uncle! A philosopher and an aesthete, he was proud of his "war machine."

"Note that it has a top speed at least twice as fast as a trotting horse: fifty kilometres an hour on flat terrain!"

When it went downhill, you can imagine…

★

Dum-dum-dum…

What do you know, it's *The Flight of the Bumblebee* now. Nela has thrown herself into the melody in the next room. That Russian music brings me straight back to my Provence. Onto the terrace, where we'd set up a brazier. Today, we'd call it a barbeque.

"The coals are perfect. Kids, go get the chops. Today's a feast day, we'll loosen our belts."

"Right away, Uncle."

Eight fine lamb chops sprinkled with rosemary. The day before, he'd gotten half a lamb in exchange for a load of fodder. For lunch, just this time, the word "blow-out" wouldn't be an exaggeration. The meat sizzled on the good coals from old vine-wood, sending up a smell that made us drool with expectation.

"Hey, Gérard! Fan it a little more."

Then, suddenly and strangely, the light waned, and a soft but constant sound made us lift our heads skyward.

"*Boudiou*, a wild swarm!"

Barely ten metres above, thousands of bees had formed a thick humming skein.

"At least six thousand! *Couquin!* Look at the size of that!"

Still remembering a bee sting barely a month earlier, I didn't linger to hear the explanations. I ran inside the kitchen, closely followed by Gérard, who quickly closed the door. Meanwhile, our uncle calmly took the time to turn the lamb chops on the grill.

"Be careful, Roger!" my mother shouted through the door.

"Don't worry. They usually don't attack when they travel as a swarm."

"But what if they do?"

"Then it's run for your lives! Look, the swarm's attached itself to the side of the roof. Everything's fine."

We ventured all the way to the threshold... then a few steps onto the terrace.

"What do we do, Roger?"

"First, finish grilling the chops, then eat them. After, I'll go get Courbon and sell him the swarm."

"But it's not ours!"

"Of course it is! A wild swarm is owned by whoever's house it resides at."

"Is it expensive?"

"Depending on its size. With Courbon, a swarm like that could go for... let's say a nice amount of flour, bread, and honey."

Monsieur Courbon was the town baker and owned several beehives. Right after our succulent meal (wisely eaten in the kitchen), Uncle went to fetch him. Our buyer carried a large burlap bag and a double ladder.

"Hello, everyone!"

"Hello, Monsieur Courbon."

"The bees are still there."

"And they'll stay a while, *pitchounet*, if I don't remove them. So I hear you were scared?"

"A little."

"Well, no need to be! They never sting when they're playing hooky."

"Are you sure?"

My mother was far from convinced.

He set his ladder against the wall and extended it: it was long enough. From his bag, he drew a thick pair of gloves and a small hood, and put them on. Then he produced a small device that looked like a miniature watering can.

"What's that?"

"That, *pitchoun*, is my censer."

"You're going to bless the bees?"

"I will, Gérard! I'll bless them and hear their confession."

"How many are there, do you think, Bastien?"

"Five thousand, five thousand five. It isn't a huge swarm, but still…"

With the help of a burning twig, he lit the substance inside the device. Thick white smoke surrounded us, much quicker than during a conclave of the Holy See, irritating our throats, noses, and eyes. Carrying a bag over his shoulder and the smoking device in his hand, which was coughing fumes in his face, Monsieur Courbon put a hand on his ladder.

"Need help, Bastien?"

"No need."

He started climbing the ladder carefully, staggering a little since he was holding on with only one hand.

When he reached the top, with a circular motion he copiously smoked the swarm and the few rebellious bees that flew around it. They quickly returned to their sisters for a deep artificial sleep. When all was quiet, Courbon took the large steaming *fougasse* of bees and stuffed it into his bag. Then, even more carefully, he climbed down the ladder.

The deal was quickly struck between Roger and Bastien. We'd get a kilo of bread every week, plus a kilo of flour and a jar of honey every month. And that, for an entire year, starting this very day. And that was how, once or twice a month, my mother became a baker herself, extending Courbon's flour with linden leaves when in season, quite rich in proteins, were we to believe Uncle Know-it-All.

★

I can still recall a few more stories from the grill. Now my memory brings forth another story, a composite: pieces of red, burning wood where blue will-o'-the-wisps dance, the thick smoke that rises from the grill, our feast that sizzles, surrounding us with the smell of the sea. Memory is like a spider web that links the disparate images in my mind.

"Ouch! It's burning hot!"

"Don't you have a knife and fork?"

I have to admit, utensils can be handy. With one sharp incision, I cut the swollen skin that barely sticks to the flesh. Firm, off-white flesh whose filets come off by themselves. Servings that I stick with my fork and easily transport to my open mouth before they break apart. And then, a gustative oxymoron, *strong and subtle*, the agreement between the sweet fennel seeds that covered the fish before it cooked and the fistfuls of sea salt thrown onto its charred skin.

Uncle brought us some handsome, slate-blue sardines.

"Where did you catch those, Roger?"

"In Draguignan."

"But there's no sea in Draguignan."

"Sure, but there's Fabre."

"Fabre, the farmer?"

"Exactly, my sweet. When I delivered the manure, he'd just come back from Fréjus where he'd traded some vegetables for a whole crate of sardines."

Uncle was proud of his expedition. This time, there was no mad swarm to disrupt our Agape, only joy this early evening, under the sweet shelter of the old linden, at the hour when the cicada orchestra brings its concert to a close. Only two or three members ignore the conductor's *pianissimo*, wanting to tune their instruments, most likely, for tomorrow's run. Time stops and peace descends upon the night. In darkness, memory fades.

❧ NINE ❧

The three little rooms upstairs were our very own Ali Baba's cave. In the nooks and crannies we found all sorts of disparate objects that had been broken or mistreated by previous generations, although no one had the courage to throw them out. We found accoutrements of the Church (a nacre rosary, a phosphorescent statuette of the Virgin Mary, a Christ medallion), assorted pieces of old Moustiers pottery (all chipped), and a jewelry box (empty) made of sandalwood with the *Normandie*, the gleaming French steamer from the thirties, painted in relief on its lid – my favourite object because of its rough paint and faint camphor smell. And a good collection of some twenty lead soldiers, Gérard's favourites, with which I'd very rarely get to play.

One afternoon, I went downstairs to complain about that injustice to my mother. She bawled him out generously from down on the terrace. Instead of giving me the Napoleon brandishing a broken sword that I'd asked for, reluctantly and with just enough strength to make it difficult for me to catch, he threw me a cavalry officer whose horse had a bent front right leg. I tried to catch it, I missed, and it bounced off my face, opening a centimetre-long gash on my eyebrow, a war wound I still carry today.

Then my mother sang in her beautiful clear voice:

> *Five little soldiers standing in a row,*
> *Three stood straight and two stood so;*
> *Along came the captain and what do you think?*
> *They all stood straight as quick as a wink.*

Her clever teasing dried my tears, and a cotton swab soaked in oxygenated water staunched the gushing hemorrhage. Then she stuck on a plaster that covered most of my eyebrow. "*Maman*, I'm disfigured with this plaster! It hides half my forehead. I can't go to school like this tomorrow." Slightly sheepish, Gérard didn't attempt any sarcastic remarks, and he settled for a half-smile.

Uncle Roger came to visit us a few hours after this misadventure. He silenced my jeremiads. "Let's fix that up. Mimi, lend me your eyebrow pencil."

My mother sharpened the pencil and handed it to Roger.

"Come over here, war hero! The plaster is skin-coloured, you can barely notice it. Don't move, we'll make you a *trompe-couillons*." With his tongue stuck out, he applied a line of pencil on the plaster, giving my intact eyebrow a twin brother.

That's how he was, our uncle, full of tricks and solutions. While he was at it, he reset the horse's leg by heating it over a candle. He said to Gérard, "You're an artist, go get us your box of poster paints." And he painted the reset leg a nice pale yellow.

"Not pale yellow. For a horse, you say 'dun'."

"Dun, like a Viking's house?"

"You got it, mister."

My mother didn't know that either. Uncle baptized the horse "Honey-Hoof." Afterward, the horse that had been at the centre of a bloody event became our favourite among the four others that comprised our imperial guard.

Some thirty years later, I had quite a surprise when, in the streets of Marseille, I heard the word *trompe-couillons* used as a synonym for the kind of make-up that conceals more than it improves. Had Roger heard it before 1944, or had he invented the word? He was the kind who could make words up. Despite my frequent visits to the racetrack, I never met a horse named Honey-Hoof. I would have certainly bet the farm on him.

Our uncle had given us all sorts of words like that. He was a real wordsmith – his *sapès*, of course, and also the wonderful verb *pastignoler,* which described Tavé the gamekeeper's hesitant steps as he left, at one in the afternoon, the Bar du Relais after having drunk his usual dose of rosé and a few licks of pastis. "I want a Casa, Tadidumdidum, gents and broads, and nothing else!" "No, sir, a glass of '51's the only one that don't hurt *dégun*!" As for Mathieu, who mended the roads, his drink was Pernod. To each his own. *Pastignoler:* a wonderful portmanteau word combining "pastis," the name of the French liqueur flavoured with aniseed; the name of Marcel Pagnol, a native of Aubagne in the Bouches-du-Rhône *département*, a playwright and author who wrote in a simple, colourful tongue, and at the end, a drop of *gnôle*, or hooch, the strong, often home-brewed alcohol made of fermented fruit or food-stuffs.

★

"*Couquin de pas Diou*, that's my bike! Hey, you, over there!"

The scene takes place on the village bridge right in front of the Bar du Relais, and the time is the noonday aperitif. The bike is leaning on the bridge railing, right across from the bar and Tavé, his accordion pants held up by clothespins, is watching it with one eye as he leans on the bar. Roger is next to him, and Gérard and I are seated by the window, sipping lemonade.

"*Fatchi d'ènti*, my bike!" Tavé runs toward it and – "Stay here, *jobastre*! You'll get…" – listening only to his anger, crosses the street, screaming.

Two German soldiers are examining his bike, and one of them is already holding its handlebars and seat as if to climb on. They both jump when they see the gesticulating Tavé stumble toward them. But since he's staggering due to an advanced state of *pastignolade*, the soldiers greet him with a smile. Their smiles turn to laughter when they hear him speak. He's talking pidgin to them so they'll understand, poor guy! They give him back his bike, pointing out that his back tire is flat. And the scene is over – phew! Tavé shrugs, and a few friendly slaps on the back are exchanged.

Friendly, in the end, but fat as silkworms, those Huns.

"They haven't gotten aggressive in these parts, but you never know."

"We don't see them much in the village."

"Sure, but they've set up shop in Riez, and there was some trouble last Monday. There was a raid and they took four men away."

"They took two hostages in Draguignan. I hear they're going to shoot them."

Comments fly every which way. Back, and proud as a peacock for having confronted and routed the enemy, Tavé declares, "*Sian propre, lei sordat!*"

"They didn't want your bicycle?"

"No, *pécaïre!* They thought it was too expensive!"

All the same, the event may have shaken him a little: he decided he needed another tumbler of rosé and a sniff of pastis to calm his nerves.

"All right, kids, time to break bread."

A figure of speech, of course (since on that day, like many others, bread would be replaced by rutabagas), yet the expression spoke of the austerity of the times. But it was a day for celebrating anyway. First, it was Thursday, and after a morning during which we did nothing (except enjoy ourselves), we still had the whole long afternoon with Uncle, who wasn't taking to the road that day. He would use the break to work on his truck – blow in the pump, clean the spark plugs, check the tire pressure – and let us drive it. Without it actually running, of course.

"Only if you stop fighting over the wheel!"

"Of course, Uncle. But I get to be first because I'm the first born."

"More like the first shorn! Bah! Bah!"

"Shut up, sheep brains!"

All in all, a wonderful morning. Then, in the afternoon, a soap bubble competition!

"Before we begin the contest, we have to build a bubble maker."

"*Qu'es aco*, Uncle?"

"A bit like a *lorgnon*…"

"And what's a *lorgnon*?"

"A kind of *fadòli* like you!"

Uncle wheeled around. "Don't start up again, or there'll be no contest!"

He wasn't joking. He said to my mother, "Mimi, I'm taking just a little piece of soap."

"Please, Roger, I hardly have any left!"

"Just a splinter, a whisker, barely bigger than your fingernail – a tiny little finger that's so small, so pretty, that I love, that I kiss."

He'd kissed it, all right. Uncle Roger always got what he wanted with my mother. And more often than not, their theatrical squabbles would end in a song, always the same one, which he'd sing as he took her by the waist and led her, swaying, onto the kitchen dance floor:

> It is you, my chérie,
> The prettiest in town,
> You are my honey
> Who makes me go 'round!

A twisted piece of wire with a round opening fashioned at one end: our device was ready to be tested. Outside, on the terrace, a sea of bubbles of all shapes and sizes floated in the air, iridescent in the last rays of the setting sun.

"Next Thursday, if I'm not working, we'll make a kaleidoscope! You'll see, it'll be even better!"

And it was. His eye fastened to the peephole of Uncle's new invention, Gérard thought he could see fish – silver ones swimming in schools, very close together, sardines and anchovies, then other kinds, more agitated, red and blue, playing among yellow and green-tinged algae. When it was my turn to look into the kal, the kali, the kalo (how do you say it? I'll never get it!), I saw exactly the same thing. Yet I'd never put my head under water, in the sea. In fact, I'd never even been to the beach.

❧ TEN ❧

In my family, everyone sang, and sang in tune. Everyone but us two bullfrogs: Gérard and I. Uncle Roger, with his lyric tenor voice that was very close to Uncle Émile's, had no trouble being accepted in the family choir.

Moustiers. The village saint's day, September 1943. On the day of the singing contest, a platform was set up on the square in front of the church, flagged and garlanded by a sea of holly, ivy, and rosemary branches. Uncle Émile and Aunt Marie sang a duo:

> *Good morning, my dear lady*
> *Good morning, my dear man*
> *I can't see you but I can understand...*

Techno before its time: they each carried a handset, which gave them a certain countenance, except when Uncle, swept away by his own enthusiasm, hit himself in the nose with the headphones. A true stoic, the perfect Marseille harbour fireman, he didn't miss a beat or drop the melody, which might have compromised their chances.

First prize: Émile and Marie!

Two years in a row.

Yet the following year, not as a duo: Émile and Marie, both finalists, faced each other in combat, never seen before.

Uncle Émile began with the perfect song for the occasion – a comical number:

> To get to my new job
> I bought a brand new car
> I swear it was no slob—
> The fastest on the road by far...

This was in July of 1939. Come September, he left for the war...

> Eight months later I come back
> Requisition: my car's become a cart...

Inexorably, the unlucky streak continued. Uncle Émile acted out pulling a large stack of bills from his pocket and bought, one after the other: a motorbike – no more gas; several bicycles – all stolen. He tried the subway – soon closed to save electricity. He made do with a good pair of shoes to make the trip four times a day – soon, no more soles. To top it all off, the cobbler ran out of leather...

> *But I'm a prudent and discerning man*
> *For tomorrow I'll have played my hand—*
> *You got it; I'll be walking on them*
> *To go see my mother, brother, and friends.*
> *And, sure, the world will be upside down*
> *But it might be funnier this time 'round:*
> *After all I've got nothing to lose*
> *Right side up, it's been giving me the blues.*

The jury laughed till it cried. Gérard lapped it up.

Aunt Marie replied with the latest success (the word "hit" didn't exist yet):

> *What is left of our love?*
> *What is left of days gone by?*
> *A picture, an old picture*
> *Of my youth.*
> *What is left of our love letters?*
> *Of springtime, and our moments together*
> *[…]*
> *Happiness withered, hair in the wind…*
> *Stolen kisses, dreams undone…*
> *What is left of it all?*
> *Please tell me.*

The jury was in tears: first prize was a tie!

To satisfy the public who begged for more:

— Good morning, my dear lady
— Good morning, my dear man…

Marseille, the fall of 1945. The radio was finally free, and everyone was basking in the euphoria of the Liberation. Sunday mornings, I remember it well: Aunt Henriette would do the weekly housework, scrubbing everything hard as she listened to "Listeners' Request" – people who'd call in to ask for *La Petite Diligence* or *Sombreros et mantilles*, for their favourite Pierre or their sweet Pierrette. A bit of dusting the furniture, the cabinet, the wireless set, the edges of the paintings, the large cabinet mirror; then up the stepladder to dust the top of the cabinet. Rub, rub, frenetically, rhythmically – *The little stagecoach / From here to the days of old* – the red kitchen tiles, the black and white ones in the corridor, the oak parquet in the bedrooms. "Don't come in, Nico, it's still wet!" *I'll wait day and night / I'll wait forever…*

As she prepared the Sunday feast, Grandma would join the chorus:

Ramona
I dreamed a beautiful dream!
Ramona,
We travelled together, my queen…

Ah! A glass of white wine we drink
In the shade of the arbour we think…

Oh, her feet were as small as can be,
Valentine! Valentine!

How much joy these songs brought! "Never again," they seemed to say. Which goes to show…

My cousins, a few years later. Lili, a tragic soprano: singing lessons, a professional voice, she missed out on her career because of the intransigence of a husband who refused to open his nightingale's cage. Jean, her brother: the same talent but without the effort, he dabbled in small songs, never seeing them through… Then to everyone's surprise, on the day of Jean's marriage, here comes a new one with an angel's voice: Félix, Gérard's older brother! He makes his way to the centre of the dance floor. No stage fright, no embarrassment, just composure and serenity! We're all astonished: how is it possible? Where has he been hiding that voice? He does Montand, thumbs hooked under his suspenders for effect, loose-limbed, strolling down the *Grands Boulevards*. And then Trénet, a real hepcat, a rose in his hat (borrowed from Henriette), rowing in *La Mer*. In Pigalle, Ulmer meandering, clippity-clop, with his friend Dudan. Borrowing an Italian straw hat from Virginie, Mireille, on vacation, follows her own sweet way that hints of hazelnut. Then Alibert, who just pinched Uncle Émile's smoke, is already missing, *oh fan!* his home: *Adieu, Venice of Provence!* Trénet returns now, hatless, choked up and pale, shedding a tear for old *Ménilmontant* where long ago he left his heart. Then a final curtain call: *Douce France*! Bravo, Fèli! A revelation, a triumph!

Those songs, sung over and over, one Sunday to the next, spoke to me of my mother and Roger:

> *Oh, the blue Java*
> *The prettiest of all…*

– the one that enchants lovers, that they danced to, eyes locked, at Chez Archiloque or on the square before the church.

And they spoke of me too, in *Au Lycée Papillon*:

Student Dominique, you are tops in French History, tell me all about Vercingétorix…Mister Superintendent, I know it all by heart! And you know geography? Then name all the départements*! Mister Superintendent, I know it all by heart!*

These songs of my youth told me of pleasures to come, with *Couché dans le foin*:

> *Lying in the hay*
> *With the sunlight shining*
> *And a bird I hear singing*
> *Not too far away…*

> *I have your hand in mine*
> *And our fingers weave together…*

The songs spoke of a great journey that would change my life:

Ma cabane au Canada...

Songs that made me sad, like *Roses Blanches*:

Today is Sunday, you know
So here, my dear mother
Take these white roses
You, who love them so!
For when I'll be older...

And others, like *La Valse des Regrets*, would teach me poetry:

The organ of night
Moans to the moon
And the breeze
With its bow
Sings the waltz of regret...

The vessel softly sings
On the satin water
To where it goes, to which dream
To which uncertainty
Of destiny...

The weight of words, the power of imagery... *Gare au gorille!*
I was preparing myself for a most important meeting:

> *You'll never forget her,*
> *No, you never will*
> *The first girl*
> *You take in your arms*
> *It was a good thing*
> *(Oh, my heart, do you remember?)*

How could I forget her, haughty despite her low station –
she was a milkmaid. If only you'd known her... The girl and
the song would arrive almost at the same time, in 1953.

⤙ ELEVEN ⤚

A rainy day in Moustiers. We were upstairs, bored, with nothing to do. In the first little room where we didn't like to play – it was always colder and more humid than the other two because there was no window – we made an important discovery: on top of the old dresser was a large metal box we hadn't seen before.

It was forty centimetres long and heavy to get down. Though rusty in spots, it was still a handsome box. Its lid, with its bright red paint, impressed us. On its topmost edge, in pale blue letters set out in a half-circle, we read: OLIVE OIL SOAP. Beneath, in small yellow letters following the same curve: 100% Authentic. In the centre of the lid, in yellow capital letters as large as the other ones but running horizontally, the name of the soap-maker: FÉLIX EYDOUX. Well-centred beneath, his place of residence in small black letters: Marseille. Set between the arc and the horizontal line of the capital letters was a large oval medallion of the Virgin. On both sides of the medallion, two gold medals, head and tail, attested to the brand's fame. Beneath the name, a bird's eye view of the Eydoux soap factory – "a steam-run factory producing 35,000 kilograms of soap every day" – with three large stacks belching dark clouds of smoke that disappeared into a crystal sky, thanks to the strong wind that blew from right to left. This swell red and gold chromo with pale blue highlights had everything we liked. It especially pleased Gérard who had become, since the success of his surprising landscape, the uncontested artist of the house, his ego further enlarged by my mother's constant flattery, since she was only a lowly copyist.

Once we opened the box, its contents intrigued us even more. We found headphones with their wires rolled around them and, underneath, a small black board made of an unknown material on which were attached various objects – in particular, a small glass tube containing a sort of black pebble with a bluish tinge.

"*Qu'es aco?*"

"I don't know. Uncle'll tell us tonight."

"Kids, you've discovered a crystal radio set!"

"What's a crystal?"

"It's that little thing there."

"It runs on a rock?"

"Not exactly a rock, a mineral that acts as a diode and a capacitor. The antenna is made of copper wire, and it captures the radio waves and sends them to the capacitor, which turns them into the energy it needs to read the radio signal."

"*Boudi*! That's complicated!"

"Uncle, can you make the crystal set work?"

"I might be able to."

"How are you going to do it?"

"Here we have earphones… And on the base, a series of instruments…"

"What's the base made of, Uncle? It's not wood and it smells strange."

"It's ebonite. A material made from rubber."

"But it's hard, and rubber is soft."

"Hard, but easy to drill through, and it's also a great insulator. Let's look at the instruments. Here you have…"

What a teacher our uncle was! He knew how to pique our curiosity.

"If we use it properly, with this model (it was an old 1925 "Wireless" model made by Oudin), we should be able to tune in to radio stations a few hundred kilometres from us. Maybe even the English BBC."

"Even Marseille?"

"Even Marseille. As long as we solidify the antenna. The antenna is this piece of copper wire. We'll need at least another thirty metres of it."

"Do you have copper wire?"

"No, but I do have an idea… We'll stretch it horizontally between the three rooms and mount it on the roof. We'll need another ten metres for the ground. We'll pass it through there, through the window, and tie it downstairs, on the water faucet."

"What's the ground, Uncle?"

"It's the opposite of the sky, idiot!"

"Oh, Gérard, stop it."

The illustration of the virtues of repetition: Uncle would explain and explain again, tirelessly. "I've just told you that... Clearly, you didn't understand. Listen again: this part is..." And always with the patience of a monk for whom nothing matters but the illuminating of his manuscript. He would find comparisons we could understand.

"A mineral is a combination of more than one metal – like soup that's a combination of more than one vegetable cooked together."

"But a mineral is hard, not liquid."

"No, not liquid; a mineral is solid. In the world, there are three different forms of matter, which we call its 'states.' Take water, for instance: it is liquid when you go and get it at the fountain, but it becomes solid when it freezes."

"That's ice."

"Yes, ice. When you boil a litre of water to make soup, the part that evaporates is in a gaseous state."

"That's steam."

"Steam is a gas?"

"It is water in its gaseous state."

The virtue of a well-presented digression.

"Now, when a piece of galena, the main mineral in a crystal set, detects a wave transmitted by a radio, it's like when your ear detects a sound from close up – the goat next door, for

example. Except that, with galena, the sound that it captures –
meaning the radio waves – comes from very far away, often
hundreds of kilometres."

"What's a wave?"

"It's something that moves in regular fashion. When you
throw a rock in the Courbon fountain, you see small waves
that move from the central point to the perimeter in succes-
sion. We say that they're dis-se-min-a-ting. They're waves, but
visible ones. Sound waves also disseminate from a central
point, but they are invisible; only your ears can catch them."

Science made easy. What a teacher! And, when necessary:
"Are you listening or are you sleeping? Don't give me a reason
to get mad…" The virtue of a righteous reprimand.

Today, I still remember how to work a crystal set. One of
the miracles of childhood: you remember everything that
was said, and the brain can store even the smallest details in
its young folds – the *sui generis* smell of ebonite, the indented
button under the fingers' touch, the tiny shifts of the detec-
tor on the galena, the few broken words that emerged from
the static. The taste of captured words, mulled over in our
minds as we tried to understand their meaning. I remember we
played a lot with our set, perhaps more than with any other toy,
though we were never able to capture a complete sentence –
blame the mountain behind the house. Still, considering
Uncle Roger and his technical abilities… If he'd been born
earlier, he would have invented the Swiss Army knife. Which,
just like that, would have become French.

He would often listen to *Les Français parlent aux Français*, "From one Frenchman to Another," with his brother-in-law, both crowding around the tube radio they refused to turn in at the town hall for a receipt. Starting at the end of 1943, wireless sets were *verbotten*!

Something big was happening with the Allies. While the French, who felt the noose tightening around their necks, began to think differently about their "saviour," the old Marshal.

❧ TWELVE ❧

Funny how memory works. Proust, of course... The same thing with *pistou*: when I smell its perfume in the air – just like that! – I remember it all.

A stampede through the quiet streets of a village heavy with sleep, at siesta time. "*Zou boulégan*, you're slowing us down, they're gonna catch us!"

Two kids in short pants sitting on the terrace, legs spread apart, face to face, in the shade of the linden. A hot summer day. The game consists of rolling a small ball back and forth, pretending it's a car, a motorcycle, a tank – a French tank! Block it, then send it back.

The same children, sitting at the terrace table. They're staring at an upside-down glass with a wasp inside, flying, trying to escape. No luck: it hits the side of the glass, tries to hold on, falls back down each time.

The outdoor latrines, squatters in a small roofless shed thrown up in a hurry, leaning against the side of a house. Should have thought of paper, there's only these large leaves left… Ouch, ouch! "I told you, those are nettles, smarty-pants! Bet you won't forget the name now!"

The same kids in the corner of the kitchen, playing ludo. "Hey, Gé! Look at those flies! What are they doing there, stuck together like that?"

"I can't tell you, you're too young."

"Why?"

"Look here, under my nose, you see?"

"Yeah, it's dirty."

"I'm not dirty, you stinking runt! It's my moustache."

"Your moustache… Well, it's not big, is it?"

"A little thin still, sure, but it's there anyway, which means I'm allowed to be interested in flies-stuck-together-like-that, and you're not."

And that was that.

Before Moustiers, my mind is a complete blank, a piece of paper on which nothing has been written. If I try to look back, it's as if I were disappearing into a bank of fog growing ever thicker. At first, a few vague apparitions: my maternal grandfather bouncing me on his knee as he laughed; my handsome father in his sailor uniform, wearing an unclouded smile; a naked child on a sheepskin… But nobody ever moves, and I'm the child. Pictures, only pictures, kept in the family album with others from the same period: my father in fatigues during the "phoney war," his helmet askew, back against a truck with his buddies as if posing for a Colgate ad ("Sparkling White Teeth!"). Another one of him, at the Fort of Six-Fours, next to an artillery piece, looking concentrated, field glasses in hand... I can search through every fold of my memory, not a single trace of my childhood before the summer of 1943. Only pictures, or objects found later, stories told over and over, like the wonderful "Retreat! Retreat!" story that my entire family loved to tell again and again, especially Gérard. I shouted out this call of defeat towards the end of 1942, while strolling through the pretty Pharo gardens with my family near the entrance to the Old Port. Just then, the cannons from a German battery started a firing exercise. I yelled, "Retreat! Retreat!" And ran off with my father chasing me, catching up to me before I could reach the garden gate...

If, today, I can remember the apartment in which I first opened my eyes – right above Henriette and Rose's house, with its two windows giving directly onto the veranda, their terrace, and their oblong garden shaped like a flagship, from which, down a fifty-metre cliff, your eyes could trace every street of the Saint-Victor neighbourhood leading all the way to the sea through the Catalan quarter – if I know every corner of that tiny apartment by heart, it's because I often took refuge there during my father's last stay there, from June to December of 1945.

Only the map of France pinned to the wall vaguely reminded me of something.

"What are those pins on the map, Dad?"

"They helped me follow the progression of the war."

I also had the image of his violin. Unfit for service! Once I knocked it off a chair and stepped on it for no apparent reason. I came upon it later, its soul shattered, unable to offer anything more than pitiful caterwauls. I can still see it today, its pretty orange-red colour with a ladybug finish.

As time progresses, the fog begins to lift, and once past it, the landscape becomes clearer: the sides of a mountain and the star that hangs between them; the cries of crows amplified by the echo; the scent of lavender; and voices, faces, and a clever cousin… Moustiers always comes back to me with its scent of *pistou* that reminds me of times past.

Today, Uncle didn't go out on the road; there was nothing to transport until Monday. He'll take the opportunity to work on his truck – brake pads and cylinder head to change. The work will take him through the weekend.

After the meal, he unfolds that day's *Petit Provençal*, Friday, May 26, 1944, brought to Moustiers on the noon bus. He looks at the headlines.

"The bastards! Enough is enough! We ought to hang 'em all, the whole editorial staff, along with the Doddering Old Man."

"Don't get worked up, Roger! Not when you're digesting."

"You bet! I can't swallow another one of these damn headlines: *NEW ANGLO-AMERICAN TERROR ATTACK ON FRANCE… LYON SUBURBS BOMBED AGAIN… ON THE SOUTHERN ITALIAN FRONT, THE GERMANS BREAK UP SAVAGE ATTACKS AND DESTROY SIXTY-SEVEN TANKS…*

A man of conviction, Uncle knew nothing about feelings that weren't absolute. He always preferred the pugnacity of honest speech to the half-truths of mealy-mouthed politicians.

❧ THIRTEEN ❧

On May 27, 1944, Marseille suffered its most deadly Allied bombardment – 1,700 deaths. News of it took two days to reach us in Moustiers; there were no newspapers on Sundays. No deaths in our family, only property damage. That same day, *Maman* turned thirty-two. A birthday that Roger would celebrate in his own way.

That morning, Uncle had us prepare a present, and a strange one, too: a handful of fresh walnuts that we fetched from a big tree in the lower part of the village, by the side of the road.

Uncle was beating the foliage with a stick when a small convoy of German soldiers came by – four or five trucks flanked by two sidecars fitted with machine guns – wearing fatigues, heavy helmets, and gas masks on their chests.

In the past months, the actions of the occupying army had grown in intensity, and stories were told of the terrible things they did. We were in that dark period during which, feeling victory slipping through their fingers, the Nazi chiefs stopped at nothing to reverse the tide. In the cities of the South, the

German Gestapo and French Militia[3] let loose, shooting so-called "terrorists" – more often than not, imaginary ones – on sight and executing hundreds of hostages. And in Germany, where the deported were found, the cleansing had begun; the concentration camps were turned into extermination camps. But France didn't know that yet.

As the Krauts passed by, much to our great surprise, Uncle suddenly brandished his stick and started yelling incomprehensibly. "Long live…!" Smack! The stick against the tree. "Long Live…!" Smack and smack again, he hit the poor walnut tree as hard as possible.

"Uncle's gone completely *calu*!" Gérard's diagnosis was immediate. I could hear the concern in his voice, and I was worried, too. Uncle's breathless explanations, once the trucks had disappeared and he'd calmed down, didn't really reassure us. He caught his breath and explained more slowly. I learned two new words as a result: a *gaule*, a noun meaning "a stick, a pole, often used for hitting," and *gauler*, a verb of the same family, "often used with an object designating a tree or fruit."

"A direct object!" Gérard gave me his superior look to remind me that even if the vagaries of our lives brought us together in the same classroom, I should never forget that he was in the older boys' division.

That same morning, we learned about a general who would cleanse the shame of French collaboration: Charles de Gaulle's name had been etched into our minds forever. The name already had an important place in my father's heart and, once he returned from the camps, he would unconditionally honour it during his long years in the Gaullists' ranks.

Back home, Roger's strange behaviour would be illuminated – at least to Gérard who, that night, spent a long time patiently explaining the situation so I would understand and finally fall asleep. Roger had told my mother how, when the German column passed by, he saw red and spontaneously echoed the cries and gesticulations of the courageous citizens of Marseille who, a year and a half earlier, had paraded down the Canebière, brandishing large sticks in the face of the perplexed German soldiers who had just arrived in the free zone that had become, that quickly, the southern zone.[4]

The walnuts were presented to my mother in a beautiful tin-plated box that had once contained LU cookies. Accompanied by a large bouquet of flowers – in the centre of which was a purple-blue thistle in bloom – tied together with a red ribbon that would have had a better effect if Uncle had thought of ironing it first. And then, a jar half-filled with alcohol, which must have represented a good litre of pastis that he had made from various aromatic herbs.

As *Maman* looked on curiously, Uncle made an incision in each nut with his pocket-knife and dropped them into the jar.

"My pretty, you'll have to wait a little. Your present won't be ready for another two weeks."

"You're going to make nut wine in fifteen days, and that, with no wine?"

"Not at all!"

"A homemade aperitif, then?"

"Nope!"

Mum's the word for two weeks. Then, ceremoniously, jar in hand – around which he'd tied a blue ribbon this time, perfectly ironed.

"Your gift, my princess!"

"What's he giving your mother?"

"I don't know…"

"Do you drink it, Roger?"

"No, you wear it!"

"Wear it? How?"

"Like nylons, on your legs, on special occasions. Tonight, for instance, to go dancing at Chez Archiloque."

It was a pretty little bistro by the village bridge, with a long, tree-shaded terrace that gave onto the river that leaped over rocks in small waterfalls. These days, the bistro houses a restaurant, now named *À la bonne écrevisse*. To prove their dedication to the crustacean, a large ceramic crayfish on a wooden crest looks down from the sign. And you can still dance on the terrace on fine summer nights.

"Stockings! And run-proof ones to boot!"

Maman carefully began colouring her legs. Then Uncle – rather enthusiastically, too! – took up an eyebrow pencil and drew, in a perfectly straight line, starting very high underneath her skirt, all the way down the curve of her leg. The vertical line did perfectly well as a seam. A real vamp!

· "Maybe you should colour your hair platinum blonde, too."

Uncle Roger hadn't invented the procedure, a well-known one, but his success with my mother was no less heartfelt.

ఌ FOURTEEN ఍

Heavy clouds over France. Since the June 6th landing on the Normandy beaches, the invader, fearing a second landing from the Mediterranean that would flank them, increases his pressure.

Everywhere, in cities and villages, people suffered terrible reprisals. Like in Oradour-sur-Glane. Saturday, June 10, 1944, at eight in the morning, when tanks entered the village located seventeen kilometres from Limoges.

The hay had just been cut, the barns were chock full of it. Around the village, a group of soldiers beat the surrounding fields to push the citizens towards the centre. The soldiers were calm and told the villagers they were there for a simple identity check. The villagers, not knowing they were facing special units that had recently distinguished themselves in Russia in the art of civilian extermination – the armoured division SS *Das Reich*, of infamous name – offered no resistance.

By early afternoon, the entire population had been rounded up on the fairgrounds, including students under the supervision of their teachers. The men were separated from the women and children, then divided into six groups. They were escorted to the hay-filled barns. Grenades were thrown inside. Machine gunners posted around the barns mowed down any would-be escapees. The women and children were brought to the church. Explosives and hay were set in the nave. More machine gunners in front of the doors...

In total, 642 victims, including 246 women and 207 children. Only five men and one woman would miraculously survive the massacre.

In the countryside, violence raged. Like the battle of the Vercors, where resistance fighters were shelled by low-flying Fock Wulfs 190s and Junkers 88s with their painted swastikas. They were surrounded and assaulted from July 21 to 24 by the Alpen, the infamous Bavarian alpine battalion, specially trained for mountain operations.

Before the Provence landing, the Vercors plateau was to be used as a deployment zone for paratroopers who'd be dropped behind enemy lines. Three thousand resistance fighters without heavy weaponry defended the position: more than nine hundred dead among them and the surrounding civilian population.

But Provence would not be outdone. Jo, who'd eluded capture in the May 1943 arrests and would later turn up in the Sainte-Baume hills, told us how, one month before the second Allied landing, the Germans would execute, once again with the utmost savagery, twenty-nine members of the Provençal

Resistance cell – André Aune ("Berthier" or "Marceau"), Albert Chaba-non ("Valmy"), Paul Codaccioni ("Kodak"), Jules Moulet ("Bernard"), the Barthélemy brothers, who gave their glorious names to two streets in Marseille, and others as well from neighbouring *départements* that they honoured through their valorous sacrifices.

"Ratted out, arrested and sent to Rue Paradis. No doubt tortured, then sent on a ride in a truck to that little valley between Signes and Cuges. I was a few kilometres from there. Our cell was aching for a fight and we were ready to take it to the Krauts, who were probably losing faith in their rotten regime… They forced them to dig their own graves! Our brave boys were belting out *La Marseillaise*! We were told all this by the only witness, a lumberjack from Cuges, Maurice Percivalle, who was working near there."

Today, the mass grave of Signes, located in the Valley of Martyrs, is a national necropolis where, on the 18th of July every year, a touching ceremony, which I attended twice during the 1970s with my Popaul, takes place.

"Executed one after the other, slowly, without a blindfold. And without the *coup de grâce*, as we were able to determine from the bodies – mouths open, hands full of dirt, fingers digging into the bloody mud… Less than a month later, on August 12th, they were offered some company: nine new individuals shot by firing squads, probably executed by the same soldiers with the same cruelty. The bastards! The valley hadn't been chosen by accident; they knew there were a lot of us in the surrounding area. They thought they could dampen our patriotic spirit. Idiots!"

Some of the larger cities soon started revolting: Lyon, Grenoble, Marseille, Toulon. Marseille, whose old neighbourhoods were already flattened and its transporter bridge burned, had its port mined – ready to blow… The battle would be a terrible one.

Without a word, Uncle Roger decided to leave. On July 29th, he went to Toulon with his brother-in-law.

"I knew it, *vaï*, that you'd leave, too…"

"*T'en faguès pas*, Mimi, I'll be careful! But I have to defend my home," he explained.

My mother returned to her nightly sobbing, and the home front recovered its old sadness.

"Here we go again! She's crying again, your poor mother!"

"I know. She isn't very lucky with her men."

⁊ FIFTEEN ⁊

On August 15th, Radio Londres, the French-language program broadcast by the BBC, announces that *Gaby va se coucher dans l'herbe*. A coded message: Operation Dragoon is set into motion. The Allies – helped by an important contribution by the Free French: 260,000 men, more than half of the total forces under the command of General Jean de Lattre de Tassigny – land near Fréjus. By nightfall of August 27th, Toulon is recaptured from the Germans. Marseille follows on August 28th. The occupier loses his foothold. He will be pursued and driven out of France along with the Vichy regime and its despicable motto, "Work, Family, Homeland," will never be heard again. Finally, the French will truly understand it to mean renunciation, paternalism, isolation. The truer words of the 1789 revolution will be reborn and heard once more: "Liberty, Equality, Fraternity."

Pride and fraternity? Not always.

By early September, the word "purification" is heard in conversations and is open to interpretation. After Aix, Marseille,

Riez, and many other cities of the South, Moustiers would also participate in the fashion of the day.

"Gérard, what are they going to do to those women in the truck?"

"They're going to shear them."

"Shear them? Like sheep?"

"Yes, like animals."

"And why are they going to shear them?"

"Because they went to bed with Germans."

"Germans? Like Franz?"

"No, Franz isn't German, he's from Alsace."

"But he speaks German, he even told me so. And when he speaks French, it's like he was speaking German."

"Not German, *coucourde*, Alsatian!"

"And why are they going to shear those women?"

"Are you deaf? I just told you: they went to bed with Germans. Right over there, at the Hôtel du Relais."

"I don't want them to get sheared. Lucie is on the truck. I know Lucie, she's nice. She gave us chocolate, remember?"

"It was German chocolate!"

"Well, maybe you didn't like it, huh? You even ate half my bar!"

The village bridge is swarming with people: almost all of Moustiers is there with the mayor, Monsieur Audibert, draped in his tricoloured sash. A lot of people from nearby places, too: Riez, Valensole, Puimosson, Les Salles, Bauduen, and La Palud... The truck is parked right in middle of the bridge. On the truck, sitting on chairs, exposed like strange creatures, four poor women, heads lowered, hands tied behind their backs. You'll never find an intelligent crowd, and this one is no exception. Some come closer to get a better look, from below, the way you'd look at a monkey in a cage. They stick their tongues out, thumb their noses, or make obscene gestures. Everyone talks loudly to show off and they bellow insults. Then comes the master of ceremonies.

No one had requested the services of Malou, the town hairdresser, to do the dirty work. She has too soft a touch. In any case, she would have refused. A shepherd was called on instead. He would know how to shear them without any niceties.

He looks at the women with the same benevolent eye as the one he casts upon his animals when he takes them by the back to lighten them of their load. The *forces*, which he pulls from a scabbard at his belt (the large scissors used to shear sheep) and brandishes for all to admire, were, for the young child I was, the paragon of every instrument of torture, as fearful as the poison apple given to Snow White by the wicked witch.

The sudden power he's acquired makes him mean and sadistic, as if he'd taken cruelty lessons from Himmler's SS, terminator division. Now for the first one! A sudden calm comes over the audience. The shearer stands behind the frightened woman – it's not Lucie, thank God – tilts her head roughly, chin to chest, and begins his job, cutting into the meat of it, the way he'd do with the fleece of some ordinary sheep, the way he'd trim, with a billhook, tufts of lavender. The clicking sound of steel in the silence. Then the uproar again: hysterical cries, mocking laughter, the crowd buzzes with insults and jibes.

I have to make an effort to swallow my tears. I make myself small, I hunch my shoulders, better to contain my emotions. Don't cry in front of everyone! Like my mother, I'll wait until I'm alone in my room. And don't cry in front of Gérard! He's imitating the adults, laughing out loud, happily joining in the shouted insults and jibes. Deep down, we live in two separate worlds, Gérard and I – he already on the cusp of adulthood and I still protected, for a short while at least, by the barrier of childhood. My mother has to quiet him down several times, then she drags us, him by the ear and me by my hand, far from this patriotic battleground of fallen hair.

Poor Lucie! I can still picture her crestfallen face, broken by the weight of her remorse – a face that has collapsed and been undone, that will now smile only through a fog of shame. I can ask myself all I want: did those women truly betray their husbands, their brothers, their fathers? While they were enjoying themselves, were their men resisting the barbarians, were they fighting, suffering, dying…? Wait a minute! In Moustiers, most men were happy to be sunshine patriots within the walls of their village. Among those four women, how many were widows? None. Married? Only one, Denise Lemoine: her husband abandoned her with two young children (Jean and

Martine, who went to Moustiers' elementary school in the same division with me). He went to live with another woman, an Italian... Weren't the Italians our enemies? Strange. As for the others, not even sixty years between the three of them! But, I would have been told, they still betrayed their country! That was treason? By betting on love, they gave hope to life. Okay, sure, maybe by risking a few little German bastards! Which meant that Gilbert, Lucie's baby, was a Nazi. We should exterminate him to purify our race... And if your mother had loved a Kraut instead of Roger, what would you have said? What a stupid allegation! My mother? Don't try to escape the problem. Her husband was in the hands of the SS, so sure it would have been betrayal. But those other women... Don't you remember the Germans from Moustiers who would come and take pictures from the bridge and show us photos of their families?

What would Uncle have done, had he been there and not in Toulon? Applauded or booed this appalling spectacle?

And my father, had he been there, would he have taken Paul Éluard's side?

> *Go figure why*
> *For me, my remorse was*
> *The broken woman who remained*
> *On the pavement*
> *The reasonable victim*
> *With her torn dress*

And the eyes of a lost child
Lost crown, disfigured [5]

Would he have been on the side of George Brassens, or on that of the "hair-splitters?" Like Brassens, would he have dared pick up a kiss curl from the mud and slip it into the lapels of his coat? I never asked him the question. [6]

Despite everything he suffered, I still think my father, had he been on the bridge that day, would never have sided with the "braid-cutters." Am I wrong, Popaul? Despite Juan, legless at sixteen, miraculously pulled from a crematory oven at Buchenwald by an American soldier, his two legs already gone up in smoke. I saw that Spaniard in February 1946, at the centre for deportees that my father was running at the time. He would drag himself along on his cart by furiously punching the ground. Despite all the horrors I heard him describe, my father did not believe that his fellow man was fundamentally good or evil – only capable of becoming one or the other depending on the circumstances. "The bastards and the saints are cut from the same cloth…" An unconditional optimist, he preferred to consider our species in a flattering light. He would often recount – with much enthusiasm and pride – the story of his friend Ludovic Caraco, whom I knew well. They had suffered their long travels together.

Not a bird sings out to cheer us.
Oaks are standing gaunt and bare.

We are the peat bog soldiers,
Marching with our spades to the moor.[7]
We are the peat bog soldiers,
Marching with our spades to the moor.

One day, in one camp or another, Caraco, whose faith in God was unwavering, came up with the idea, in order to get an extra bowl of soup for a friend who was in very bad shape, of betting his life by challenging an unshakable-looking guard. "If I toss my cap on the other side of the line that we aren't allowed to cross under penalty of death, and I go fetch it, you give me more soup. If you haven't shot me, of course." A harsh look, and the deal was settled with an arrogant sneer. Caraco slowly took his cap off as the German soldier sighted him. Caraco fingered the striped cap before throwing it as far as he could. The cap fell a good five metres over the line. The guard snarled and muttered something. Then Caraco, walking backwards, gazing directly into the guard's eyes, approached the line, then crossed it, leaned down... The guard's fingers tensed on the trigger. But the snarl was gone now, and his eyes were wide open. Caraco crossed back over the line, walking proudly, cap in hand, and went straight to the guard to demand his prize. He shook the German's sweaty hand. "God bless you!"

When his friends asked him why he'd tempted the Devil by throwing his cap so far, he told them the Devil could never contend with God. He explained that "He who reigns both on Earth and on Heaven" told him to toss the cap far enough to give the guard time to think. And that He took care of the rest. Another miracle on His side, if we're to believe Caraco. Those few spoonfuls of cold soup, whose contents should not be speculated on, may have saved his sick friend. Like my father and Caraco, he survived – broken, of course – and saw his native Normandy again.

❧ SIXTEEN ❧

"Are you ready, Dominique? Time to go to Nova Era!"

"Just five more minutes, Nela."

They're always tasty, those *bifanas*! We return home, loaded with a pound of dough (for the *oreillettes* that Nela will make based on Aunt Henriette's recipe) and a variety of breads: ultra-light *caraças, pão saloio*, heavy and compact, and *pão de milho*, even more compact – an acquired taste, made from maize). And a small cake, a *toucinho do céu* (sugar, eggs, butter, and crushed almonds – impossible not to love).

Back home and not even four o'clock. Two hours to relax: Nela at her piano; me in my office. Where, once again immersed in memories of childhood, with the scent of *pistou* wafting through the house, I return to my daydreaming, travelling back through the years.

★

Tonight, like yesterday and the day before, we speak few words. We have gathered around the kitchen table, under the lamplight, on the edge of darkness. My mother is mending a few things, bent over her work. Sewing a button back on Gérard's grey shirt, she pulls the needle and cuts the thread with her teeth.

Not a word is spoken.

Gérard draws another mountain. Never has his eraser worked so hard, yet he should be able to draw the shape of the mountain with his eyes closed by now.

"You aren't drawing the star?"

"No."

"Why?"

No answer.

I go back to *Big Bill*. *Big Bill, le casseur*: the bee's knees! It came by bus yesterday and I've been re-reading it ever since. Aunt Henriette discovered this new comic book when she went to buy her paper. Big Bill is a lawyer in a small town in the Far West – a lawyer for the downtrodden who never makes his clients pay. And he can afford the generosity, being the owner of a huge ranch with plenty of horses, thousands of head of cattle and a few dozen cowboys at his service. Big Bill is a real giant: his biceps are at least twice as big as Uncle Roger's. And the size of him! Bill's shirt would billow around Uncle Roger like a flag. But Bill wouldn't hurt a fly. Except when he puts on his red shirt, his black mask, and picks up his whip to punish the bad guys. When that happens, Evil-Doers beware! And nobody recognizes him except his horse Silver and me. Gérard doesn't like Big Bill; he says he's "full of hot air" and calls him Big Butt and "butter-dish breaker." But he only says that to annoy me, because he reads every new issue down to the last page.

Pretty soon I'll have at least thirty issues: once a month adds up fast. All of them lost, by now, gone up in smoke in Roger's garage, in Aubagne, at the end of the forties: he used to use them to start his gasifier! I'd gone to live with my father in Marseille to go to high school, and Uncle must have thought I had better things to read than some kiddie magazine that probably didn't interest me anymore. The truth is that I mourned them for a long time and looked for them in every bookstore in Marseille until I started university. I would have gladly traded Camus' *The Stranger* or Sartre's *The Words* for them. At least those books would have been easier to find again.

That Roger! He was the cause of our silence in the summer of 1945. We had no news of him for a long time – forty-seven days, to be precise.

★

Finally, *doe gratis*! In mid-September, Uncle Roger returned from the war, overflowing with compliments and a flower in his gun. The fight was hard, we heard. But he didn't like speaking about it in front of us, the children.

The horizon brightened. Once again we could be filled with wonder at the blue waves of the mountains. We celebrated his triumphant return. On the terrace table, homemade jam, apple pie, cool, silky water (brought by Gérard from the nearby spring) and "national coffee" – an infusion of acorns sweetened with saccharine. Our faces began to glow again.

"What do you say we play a little *belated*, all four of us, Roger?"

"The kids know how to play?"

"Of course, Uncle."

"And you, Dominique?"

"Yes, but not with four people."

"It isn't hard, you'll see."

Indeed, not hard at all. After a few practice rounds, I was playing as well as the others, according to Uncle, who was satisfied with his new partner. I played my hand with more and more confidence, and my voice dared participate in the conversation particular to card players: "Trump, I cut it: eight of clubs! I'll raise it: ten! Discard: jack of hearts!" From time to time, I needed a little encouragement: "All right, it's your turn, Nicou!" Gérard, carefully watched, had to swallow his light-hearted jibes.

"*Belated, rebooted*, last card!"

My mother concluded the round with panache, then counted their total. "Don't forget the *belote*, Auntie." Gérard, from the older boys' division, added up the points on a small piece of paper, counting them on the fly. "We won, Auntie: 1060 to 780!"

The let-down of defeat. But there was no time to be sad, as Uncle announced excitedly, "Now that I've taken my old rifle from its case, we'll go hunting, kids! We'll be eating meat soon enough."

For four long years, Roger had hidden his rifle from the authorities. He hadn't waited for the Vichy regime to fall to start setting traps and snares and giving us the chance to taste, whenever he could, a few thrushes or hares. But now, as he said with great conviction, "*Fan de chichourle*, let the bullets fly!"

In the *département* of the Basses-Alpes, hunting season officially opened on the first Sunday of October 1944.

✌ SEVENTEEN ✌

"The moon is wearing a halo, so tomorrow will be a beautiful day. We'd better go to sleep if we want to be up by dawn." Gérard is first in bed, no complaints. The prospect of tomorrow's hunt completely pacified him. On the surface, at least; I'm certain that under his calm exterior, he's as agitated as a bag of cut snakes. Truthfully, between him and Roger, I don't know who's the most impatient. Uncle probably, since he's been waiting for this day to come for a long time. Finally, hunting season has opened.

I was about to turn eight, of age to participate in the hunt, too. The week before, Malou had cut my hair and given me the same look as Gérard. But nothing was certain yet: my mother still had to be convinced. Uncle Roger managed to be persuasive enough – perhaps not that hard a task considering that my mother never refused him anything.

"Don't you think he's still a little young to go hunting?"

"Of course not! He's tireless, always running everywhere!"

"Exactly. He could do something stupid, get lost or fall into a gully…"

"He's a good kid, he never disobeys. Isn't it true, Nico, you won't stray far from me?"

"No, Uncle, promise!"

"And if you come upon a German, hiding in the bush?"

"Bah! They're all gone, the Germans."

I answered as quick as a torpedo, as much to reassure myself as my mother.

"If we do see a German, he'll get it for sure! Uncle'll have his twelve-gauge with him!" Gérard added.

"But I think we'd have trouble fitting him into the game pouch."

Uncle chose laughter to sweep away my mother's fears. And it worked.

Gérard was asleep in a second. I barely had time to put my pajamas on. Curled in a ball, nose in his pillow, he was already snoring away.

Roger had just put on his coat and was getting ready to return to his house. But as often happens, he decided the time was ripe for a good prank. This time, Gérard would be his victim. My mother seemed a little worried.

"Nico, put a sweater over your pajamas and put your hat on."

"Why?"

"Shush, you'll see."

Hat on, he motioned me to follow him into our room where Gérard, on his stomach, was snoring loud enough to deafen us, sounding like a motor with a broken piston.

"Get-up, kiddo," Roger told him. "We'll be late because of you."

"Huh, what? I'm coming!"

Putting his money where his mouth was, Gérard sat up for a moment on the edge of his bed, rubbed his eyes, then, *bang!* completely exhausted, he solemnly turned his back on us and buried his face in his pillow.

When the alarm rang at five in the morning, he came to wake me up. My mother, still a little upset, decided she would stay in bed and not get involved in our preparations.

At exactly quarter past five, Roger knocked at our door, dressed for the occasion, neatly resembling Nimrod, minus the moustache. Since my mother really didn't get up, it was up to Uncle to make breakfast, a rather frugal one at that: a slice of greyish bread with a thin spread of ersatz margarine, dipped in a bowl of ersatz coffee sweetened with saccharine, lightened with a drop of milk that at least came from a real goat. Then he made lunch: the same bread, sliced thicker though, and a large piece of ham and rind, looking so tasty Gérard and I started salivating. Uncle had a way of finding things. The meat came from Hamel the butcher, whose son Jules was a child-hood friend.

"Gérard, you'll carry the game bag. It's light, there's only the canteen in there. But when we return, *daïse!* It'll be much heavier, I guarantee that!"

"But when we return, Uncle, we'll have drunk all the water."

"You, Nico, you'll be responsible for the *biasse* with our lunch and the three apples. It isn't heavy."

He meant the blue haversack that was used to carry food back from the market. We had two like it, but one was enough for today's hunt.

"Yes, Uncle, I'll take care of the *casse-graine*. You can even put a bottle of wine in it."

"That's a great idea!"

"There's a half-bottle in the cupboard. It's the one you brought over last week."

"Hmm, let's see. That should be enough. I'll fill this smaller bottle with it."

"But for the three of us, one canteen won't be enough!"

"Hey, smarty-pants, there'll surely be some springs along the way… I bet Uncle knows where they are."

"You're right, Gérard. There are at least four on our hunting grounds."

My imagination soared at the sound of those words. Our own hunting grounds! Uncle sure was swell.

Finally, we were ready! The preparations were done and we were eager to get going. "On the road, hop-toad!"

We headed off in single file – Gérard first, Uncle closing the march, and me sandwiched in between. That way, my mother, who was spying on us from the window, thinking we hadn't seen her, would be reassured and go back to bed.

We quickly climbed the slope in front of the house, and soon we were treading the Riou road. We walked past Cousin

Marcel's garden and then passed through the village's old fortified gate. "An arch mounted with a fifteenth-century dripstone," the very voluble Roger explained to us, virtually quivering with enthusiasm and sputtering with impatience. We reached the Riou waterfalls with its giant swimming holes that we loved to dive into, sometimes sensing a trout brushing against our feet... The falls fell away behind us. We barely noticed the swimming hole today.

In the sky, the slow circling of cawing crows.

"You don't hunt those birds, Uncle?"

"No, Nicou, not crows. The meat is tasteless and tough. They aren't worth the price of the lead."

"Hey, bumble-head, don't you remember anything?"

"You, Gérard, don't you start."

Of course I remembered. On a cold day last winter, when we were particularly hungry, Uncle resigned himself to hunting crows, bare-handed. He had come this way, where they were forever circling over the rocks, and had brought back one that barely weighed half a pound. He had caught it in its nest after climbing a steep cliff and killed it by choking it with its own wing. "Just one. But it wasn't easy to go get them so high up," he apologized, laying his haul on the kitchen table. *Maman* plucked it and thrust the poor thing into a *court-bouillon*. Gérard was the first to offer his opinion: "Ick!"

"I told you, Mireille," Roger said, "it's tough meat, and it doesn't have much taste." Mother agreed, decreeing that such a mere pittance wasn't worth the danger involved in fetching it. We ate with little enthusiasm. But Gérard refused the dish, declaring, "Yuck, it's worse than rutabagas!" In those times of permanent privation, when my mother would perform daily miracles to provide us the strict minimum for survival, my cousin, the son of a dyed-in-the-wool gourmet, often elegantly turned up his nose on our feast.

A few more steps and we reached the side of the mountain, in the midst of thick, acrobatic olive trees, twisted around the rocks. Higher still than the church steeple. Down below, Moustiers was making the most of its last hours of sleep. A milky sky above us. To the east, the sun was clumsily beginning to add some colour: its streaky red lines bled over the silhouette of the distant hills. The moon, translucent like a jellyfish, had not yet left the frame.

We had been climbing the steep slope for a while now. Uncle Roger was in the lead, his gun on the inside of his elbow. "Stay behind me!"

A little later: "Kids, look at the hawk!" Up in the expanse of the sky, gliding majestically, perfectly horizontal, almost stationary, as if the bird of prey were hanging by a wire.

"Are you going to shoot it?"

"No, it's too high. But if it's staying around here, it means there'll be better things waiting for us."

Indeed. A furtive rustling in a neighbouring thicket and – just like that! – a golden pheasant practically flew between our legs and lifted noisily into the air. Two loud shots. Stopped in mid-flight, the heavy bird fell earthward, twenty metres away, like a shining meteor. A few steps and Gérard was on it, brandishing the trophy over his head. A good way to start!

Annoyed, the hawk glided farther away. Suddenly, the wire broke and the black shape dove straight into the valley.

During our two-hour walk, we made our way through olive trees and terraced vines, broom beds, rosemary tufts, small forests of green oaks, two or three pine-wood stands – my first botany lesson, all of it well described by Uncle and echoed by Gérard, who showed an unusual degree of patience towards me. We also came across a pheasant (in Gérard's game pouch), a hare (still running), two rabbits (the second, of the beautiful pre-myxomatosis variety, a good four pounds of lean meat, keeping company with the pheasant), and two flights of young partridges – my first zoology lesson. Uncle waited a bit too long before shooting, and the entire squadron flew off right under our noses.

Two good catches in two hours: our hunt seemed to be going well. And it would get better. By the end of the day, we added a woodcock, a blackbird, and a dozen *sanguins*, those mushrooms you find at the foot of pine trees and that secrete brick-red sap when you break them open. "Well, a rather nice opening day, no?" Uncle Roger declared. "Though I would have liked to bring back a partridge!"

But the most salient memory of that wonderful day is neither the abundant harvest of new words and new things, nor the well-stocked game-sack, nor the odour of gunpowder that I can still smell today, nor even the deafening din of gunshots and the subsequent buzzing in my ear, it was – marked forever by the seal of infamy – our spoiled picnic that was all my fault.

Around seven-thirty, thirst forced us to take a short break. In less than a minute, we drank down the entire contents of the canteen. "There's a spring about five hundred metres away. We'll stop there, have a bite to eat and fill the canteen."

We started walking again. We had almost reached the top of the slope, and the walk was easier. Up ahead was a small stand of pine that sent its perfume wafting towards us. Uncle, hand shading his eyes, got his bearings. "This way, we're almost there."

He was right. Soon we found ourselves in front of a tiny stream, sparkling between two rocks like a viper; we could have walked right by and missed it completely. "*Daïse, Daïse, pitchounets*! Not so fast!" With a stick, Uncle beat the grass around the stream. "Asps love the freshness. Okay, now you can go." We made for the stream, lapping up the cool, clear water.

Even in Moustiers, I had never tasted water so delicious. Water for happy days – even better than the kind Uncle slipped me from time to time, with a few drops of pastis in it, when my mother wasn't looking.

"And now, let's have a bite!"

I opened our precious *biasse* that I had guarded and protected all the while. How dreadful! It was full of dirty clothes!

"And what are we going to eat now, idiot?" Gérard said to me in a rage.

This time, I had no answer.

"You see, his mother was right. We should have left the little snot at home!"

I swallowed my tears and tried to hide my shame.

"How did this happen, *moun bèu?*"

"I don't know, Uncle..."

"Where did you take this *biasse* from?"

"From the hook, near the chimney."

"That's not a hook, idiot! That's a peg for clothes!"

Gérard wasn't done with me yet.

"Didn't you see that I'd hung the other bag on the chair?"

"I don't know, Uncle…"

"That's all you have to say?"

Sheepish, indeed, for that was all I had to say.

"What are we going to eat now?"

Gérard was worried. But he shouldn't have been, because Uncle was always full of ideas.

"Let's keep walking. Higher up, we should find Antonin the shepherd."

"*Pau-Parlo?*"

"Yes, *Pau-Parlo.* I'm sure he'll have something to nibble on."

Another half-hour of walking on an empty stomach. The vegetation grew sparser and the trees gave way to meagre pastures, studded with small flowers. Far away, sheep and goats stood in the grass, not unlike a manger scene.

"Tell me, Uncle. Is that black dog over there mean?"

"No, that's Riquet, he knows me."

I was happy that Gérard had asked the question and especially happy he had asked it before me. And relieved at the answer. As predicted, Riquet bounced over to us with a friendly wag of his tail. He came and licked Uncle Roger's hand. Uncle kneeled down to converse with the dog and introduce us. Riquet approached, head down, to sniff our legs. Uh-oh, his tail stopped… But all's well: he just needed time to wind up the machine again and his tail started wagging allegretto.

"Hey, Tonin!"

The man sitting in the shade of a small tree answered without getting up.

"*Adiéu, coulègo!*"

We walked towards him, escorted by Riquet, whose good intentions could be read in his tail.

"The hunt's brought us here… Been a while, eh?"

"*Coumprèni qué!*"

"Gérard, open the game-sack. Look inside, Tonin!"

Antonin raised his arm halfway to show his admiration. But having unlearned speech from his constant solitude, he didn't add words to his gesture.

"You better believe it's not over yet."

"*Belèu.*"

Maybe. Not an optimist, the shepherd. He must not know Uncle well enough.

"Took us almost three hours to get here…"

"*Tres ouro?*"

"We went by Courbon's olive trees to get away from the rest of the pack. You better believe they're shooting down near Ducasse's land."

"*Li a de lèbre, au dabas.*"

"*Sàbi, maï…* with the kids, it isn't safe."

Close up, the man looked much older than Uncle Roger. Almost as old as the landscape: his face gullied, his features chiselled, and a thick white moustache.

At his feet, a sheep that had been sleeping got up, walked a few steps away, then stuck its nose in the grass. We sat down. It was good to rest in the shade after all our effort. Calm settled over me – but not my stomach, which growled hungrily and accused me of neglect. But soon it would stop complaining. Not just because of Antonin's gifts – he offered each of us a small sheep's-milk cheese, dry, the way I like it, and a large piece of dark bread, almost as hard as the cheese – but because of a small detail that repelled me from my first bite and ruined my appetite for the rest of the day.

Antonin chewed, which meant he stuffed a large piece of tobacco into his mouth and, just like a sheep, ruminated it with care, moving it from one side of his mouth to the other with a grimace that twisted his jaw and made the silver hairs of his beard stand up. The thorn in my side, if I can put it that way, was that, after a few minutes of meticulous mastication, he started spitting out large wads with the regularity of an aerial barrage. With strength and precision, his spit hit a flat rock a few metres away, once white, but now turning yellow. But he spat carefully: we never came under fire from his barrage.

I can't find the words to depict Gérard's half-hidden look of disgust (my cousin always had a refined appetite, and even a year of army grub in the Algerian Aurès could not discipline it).

I discreetly made my food disappear, even the fig that was supposed to be my dessert, into Riquet's open and available mouth; I could swear the dog winked at me.

Uncle didn't seem to notice. His voracious jaws stopped only to maintain the conversation that so far had been more like a monologue.

"Been here a while, Tonin?"

"*Un pau.*"

"A few weeks?"

"*Vinto-sèt jou.*"

"You'll stay here how long, then?"

"*Jusco lei proumiés jou d'ivèr.*"

That would be the final confidence of our loquacious friend who, as we were getting ready to leave, bestowed a half-smile on us and touched his cap with two fingers. "*Adessias,* Tonin!"

The sun was high in the sky now, and it was past noon by the time we got back on the road. It would take us two hours to return to Moustiers, and we'd promised my mother to be back by early afternoon. She must already be worried.

A pheasant, a nice rabbit, a woodcock, a blackbird, a dozen pine mushrooms, a large head of thyme, marjoram, and rosemary – and, of course, the fresh air, the landscape, the emotions, and the rest – certainly made getting up for before the sun and walking twenty kilometres over rough ground worthwhile.

❧ EIGHTEEN ❧

Our lives in Provence had changed profoundly since the Germans cleared out and the war moved away, taking with it its procession of idiocies and atrocities… Although we ate just as badly, we were breathing easier. In our house, every day since Roger's return was a celebration. There was only one problem. The truces between Gérard and me never lasted long. Our squabbles were endless, sometimes outright mean, but always underscored by a certain tenderness.

"What is it this time, Dodo?"

"You're mean! You…"

"You're not going to start again, are you?"

"You never let me talk!"

"You asked me a question, right?"

"Yes…"

"So let me answer! I'll explain what the teacher told us older and wiser boys."

"Well, I heard her, too."

"Sure, the Ant is industrious, but most of all she's mean and selfish. But the Cicada isn't lazy."

"I know, she's an artist."

"She sings, that's her job."

"And also, she's generous…"

"Good job, Dodo, you got it!"

"She's paid to entertain people."

"Or help them sleep. You always sleep in the afternoon on the terrace, when the cicadas sing under the linden."

"And you don't sleep?"

"So even the younger kids in class understood what Madame Dupuis said?"

"Yes, but I'm not sure about Martine and Jean, though."

"Aren't you a smart one, Dodo! If your plumage were as pretty as your song…"

"And you, Gé, if your…"

"If my what?"

This time, he didn't interrupt me. I fell silent, with my mouth wide open like a carp trying to swallow a fly. I could not remember a single line of verse! On that day, I decided I needed to learn the magical words of Jean de La Fontaine by heart.

★

On January 6, 1945, the day after my eighth birthday, Gérard and I were invited to visit my cousin Jeanne, the wife of Cousin Marcel, Uncle Émile's first cousin. The couple lived a few minutes away from us in a large house even more rustic than ours – an old farm with a stable beside it and a yard where, all day, a dozen hens would peck at grain and scratch the ground, looking for worms. More numerous than the hens were the scrawny cats that would lie in the sun, sleeping in acrobatic poses, rolled in tight balls or showing their furry tummies.

We made our way there shortly before six, the sky already turning grey. The hens had returned to the henhouse and the cats were beginning to stretch; soon enough, in less than half an hour, night would fall like a stone, and that would be their time. Their ranks increased by others from the four corners of the town, the company of cats would begin their familiar concert. Its principal refrain would be, as always, the imitation of a baby's cry. That part of Moustiers was known as "Caterwaul Lane."

As soon as we entered the heavy front door, my nose picked up an appetizing scent that made my mouth water. In the shadows of the dimly lit kitchen, my eyes were immediately drawn to the halo of light cast by the hearth, where I could discern half-buried baked potatoes in their jackets of ash. They were crackling like firecrackers and sending up small bouquets of sparks. Gérard was already licking his chops.

A surprise was waiting for us. A door opened and in she came, as pretty as a picture, making her dress sway with her hips. It was Dany, our classmate, Madame Dupuis' daughter and our hosts' granddaughter – a distant cousin, then, by the ricochet of wedlock, since Émile was our uncle through marriage… Dany laughed loudly at our dumbstruck air, her eyes sparkling, her small nose sweetly turned up, a porcelain mouth and long golden braids: Gérard stared at her like a drowning man would a buoy. When she kissed him, his cheeks turned red.

"It's my birthday, too. I turned nine the day before yesterday. I'm a year and a day older than you."

Her blue velvet dress reached halfway down her calves.

Gérard, in an aside, said, "A shame her dress is so long…"

"Why? I think it looks good on her!"

His eyes answered me with a glint of disdain, and from then on, he did not consider me worthy of his confidences.

Our hostess seated us at the table – Dany and I next to each other and Gérard on the other side. It was a children's supper, and Cousin Jeanne served us. Ah, that great pantry with its creaking doors, its shelves bending under the weight of its provisions, barely visible but never forgotten! Cousin Marcel came and went from one room to the next. Each time he opened the door that led from the kitchen to the stable, we would get a generous whiff of the heavy *sui generis* odour of Bijou the horse, who made himself heard throughout the meal with his constant kicking against the planks of the partition.

Like all of us, Gérard had a healthy appetite, but I'm not sure he knew what he was eating. The proof: when we got back home, he let me describe the details of our meal.

"We ate so well, *Maman*! You should've seen it! We started with a boiled egg, laid that same day, with bread for dipping that Cousin Marcel cut from a giant loaf. Then Cousin Jeanne gave each of us a big piece of meat."

"It was salt pork," Gérard corrected.

"It was this thick!"

"Really?"

"Really! Ask Gérard. She cooked it on the coals with potatoes."

At our house, potatoes were only for special occasions. My mother had invented a simple way to prepare them that had earned her Roger's oft-repeated compliments. In season, she'd chop a handful of young linden leaves that she'd mix with a few drops of olive oil to make a doughy substance that we would spread on our boiled potatoes. "What a taste, Mireille! Much more delicate than thyme or rosemary!" Delicate, no doubt about that. Too delicate for Gérard – "It tastes like nothing, Auntie, just good oil!" – and I wouldn't disagree with him. But I didn't want to disappoint my mother or contradict Roger, so I deferred my quick judgment and concentrated on the more-than-subtle flavour for which, with a generous effort, I could invent a whole palette of tastes.

"They're good, these potatoes! Much better than last week's rugatabas."

"It's rutabaga, *niston!*"

"Stop that! Gérard's always looking for a fight, *Maman.* We put real butter on the potatoes and they melted in my mouth!"

"Cousin Jeanne sure spoiled you."

"She also gave us a green salad. Slightly bitter, but anyway… And to finish it off, we had a big nut cake in the shape of a heart. You should have seen it! With two candles stuck in it, a pink one and a blue one."

"You forgot the fruit and the bottle of apple juice," Gérard added, critical as always.

So he had been paying attention to something other than Dany after all. Though throughout the meal, he'd seemed hypnotized by her – especially her precocious blouse, white and impeccably ironed, lifted by two audacious peaks that obviously caught his eye more than our mountains ever could. Even if he did talk about those mountains all the time, promising to climb them as soon as possible.

The night was spent in harmless and merry talk.

When the time came to leave, Gérard rushed to kiss Dany before I could, pushing me aside with a sly elbow to the deltoid. He took her by the shoulders and held her at a distance a second, the better to admire her.

The night was thick and heavy by the time we left our cousins' home and started to make our way back, interrupting the concert of the cats. Walking in front, Gérard must have had as good vision as they did, since he came to my rescue more than once, bringing me back onto the right path with reassuring strength.

In Provence, 1945 was a year of euphoria. Our life in Moustiers had taken a serene turn. At least we had the semblance of serenity.

✿ NINETEEN ✿

My father's last station of the cross. Dachau was liberated on April 29, 1945, by units of the 42nd and 45th infantry of the 7th American Army, eighteen days after Buchenwald. Two more weeks of waiting in that hell, then evacuation to Paris and accommodation in the Hôtel Lutetia: comfortable, sure, but not yet paradise. My father thought he'd find it in Marseille.

From the Lutetia, he called Uncle Eugène's office. "Oh, brother! Oh, brother! Oh, Holy Mother of God!" Then a long silence. That's all Eugène could say to his brother-in-law come back from the dead. My father reached Marseille two or three weeks later because of medical and sanitary measures. He was carrying exanthematic typhus, which had to be treated in Paris. Eugène must have been saddened but relieved by the delay, for it gave him and the family a chance to absorb the events and ready themselves for the return of the prodigal son.

Grandmother Rose and Aunt Marie, her oldest daughter, came to Moustiers as soon as they heard the news. I was eight and half then, and though I hadn't had a chance to read Corneille yet, I understood the immense pathos of the situation, underscored by my mother alternating between tears and laughter. Aunt Marie remained silent. Gérard, too. His silence impressed me the most. Rose, as always, found the right words. She summed up the situation with clear logic that brought my mother back to harsh reality. "You must speak to Roger as soon as possible. You'll judge his reaction then. And you'll see how you yourself react. It's important for you, for him and for Paul. For now, you'll stay here with Gérard; he has to finish school. Your sister is going to stay too, and your brother-in-law will have a week off work in the harbour and he'll come on Saturday. I'm going to take Dominique back to Marseille. His father will need him. Then, when we settle him in and explain everything, it'll be your turn, daughter, to go and speak to him."

My mother almost fainted.

"Speak to Paul? How?"

"You'll do it, that's all."

"It'll be much too hard."

"Of course it'll be hard! But not complicated: you'll let your heart do the talking. In a few days, you'll see things more clearly, dear. As for you kids, you'll be separated for a few days, but only until summer vacation. Okay?"

"If we have no choice…"

His feathers ruffled, my cousin resigned himself.

"Yes, Grandma, it's okay."

My heart was broken: to leave Gérard, *Maman*, Roger...
Though we were making a big deal of seeing my father again,
I wasn't even sure I knew him.

"Don't whine, you brat."

"I'm not whining!"

"Right. You're not whining, you're crying."

As always, Gérard was aggressive, hiding behind big words.
But I could see by his face – especially his chin, trembling like
apple jelly – that he was sad, too.

"Will you miss me, Gé?"

"Runt! Who do you think I am?"

His chin trembled again.

We ate on the fly: boiled eggs, grated carrots, tomatoes
with salt. Then, *rascle* on the village bridge.

"Don't forget your bag, scatterbrain."

"*Agante, niston!*"

Gérard threw me the bag. Our goodbyes were brief. My
grandmother was already at the terrace gate.

"Come on, dear! No, Marie, all of you, you're not coming.
All right, enough tears. What will the village think of us?"

The church bell had just begun to chime when the bus left
the bridge at exactly three o'clock. The bus drove down the
swerving curves onto the plain and passed the modest wall of
hills, then came to a small city: Riez. We stopped a few minutes to pick up passengers.

The next stop was more than half an hour away. The
road started by winding through field and prairie but quickly

began to turn and twist along the edge of a deep canyon. Tight curves that scared me stiff. Finally we reached an oasis: Gréoux-les-Bains.

I stumbled off the bus, the way I would roll off a roller coaster a few years later at the carnival. My feet felt like they were walking on cotton, and my eyes tried to look everywhere at once. Barely time to make it to the ditch and throw up my meagre meal. I breathed through burning, stinging nostrils that actively participated in my internal cleansing ritual.

Finally, the ground grew firmer, the landscape more solid, each thing in its place – the bus, the people, the buildings. Even the battalion of ants besieging what was left of my lunch. Ah, the happiness of seeing things as they are! My stomach declared itself open for business again – and declared it loudly. But it would have to wait until Aix-en-Provence.

The bus pulled away with three or four more passengers. The next stop was Vinon.

Now the road was almost straight, following the left bank of the Durance River. The bus purred and I fell asleep to the sound.

Quarter to six: Aix-en-Provence, the city of a hundred fountains. A twenty-minute break on the shaded terrace of a bar on the Cours Sextius. In the plane trees, bunches of sparrows chirped. A toilet stop, a sandwich and lemonade.

Then came the long road down to Marseille, which we'd reach around seven in the evening, after travelling through Luynes, Les Trois Pigeons, La Mounine and La Malle. The road crossed open country as the sun deserted the sky. Soon, the road's straight line met its first houses: La Viste, in Marseille's shadow.

Just as we began descending a steep slope, the sun reappeared, a large red balloon floating in the clear sky. It was almost touching the horizon. Below us, Marseille tumbled into the sea. We were overlooking everything: the layers of houses, the port, and even the steeple of Notre-Dame-de-la-Garde, perched on its hill. Marseille, a boat of a city, always pushing against its moorings and heading toward open water, ready to lift anchor and sail past the islands of Frioul and Château d'If, a few cable-lengths away.

Our bus finally stopped on the square in front of the Stock Exchange, right by the Canebière and the Old Port. The place brought back no memories; without Grandma Rose at my side, I would have surely felt lost. In a hurry to get home, she took me by the arm and dragged me towards a large bar, the Brasserie des Templiers, its terrace completely packed. "Let's take the side street, on the right." And just like that, we were facing the postcard view of ancient Lacydon. I started to remember, vaguely... Yes, of course! On the hill, the Holy Mother was still there.

In Moustiers, I'd hear Gérard exclaim, "Oh, Holy Mother of Marseille!" My mother and Roger, even if he was a native of Toulon, said the same thing, as did more than a few inhabitants of Moustiers. Oh, Holy Mother – even Jésus had picked that one up.

What a racket, what an uproar! People singing, shouting, calling to one another, arguing.

Never in Moustiers had my eardrums suffered such aggression. Except when Roger would shoot off his gun next to me. And these smells of salt, iodine, pitch, and fish: Marseille had its own odour, different from the scrublands of the lower Alps. A *miéterrane* scent (a beautiful Provençal adjective brought into French by the writer Suarès). Through all my senses, I was rediscovering the city of my birth.

We crossed the wide street in front of us that Grandma called Rue de la République, and we found ourselves in front of another bistro, this one even more packed than the first, with tables jostling for room with the passersby on the sidewalk.

Ten years later, the *Samaritaine* (I didn't know the name at the time), from which your eyes can wander all the way from the Quai des Belges right up to the wonderful Notre-Dame-de-la-Garde, would become one of my preferred spots. I would often stop by, accompanied by Suzon, Martine, Maryse, Éliane, or Mimi, and drink everyone's favourite. "*Garçon!* Two rum-pineapples." A dose of pineapple syrup, a shot of rum, lots of water and ice. The same colour as Ricard, but with a far superior taste – that of adolescence.

We quickened our pace and made our way towards the Quai des Belges. Just as we were crossing a street, an American Jeep zipped past at top speed only an inch from us. Grandma Rose, never one to mince words – she was a fishmonger, after all – yelled, "Hey, Blackie! You liberate us yesterday and run over us today?"

At the head of the quay, fishermen were mending their nets, using both bare hands and feet.

In the middle of it, the impressive grey silhouette of a US Navy ship hid the waters behind it. "Grandma, it's swarming with people here!" There were military men everywhere, especially Americans speaking a strange tongue. GIs wearing khaki, sailors in navy blue and funny white hats. I wanted to linger in front of the warship, but Grandma was pulling me by the arm. "Come on! The tram is already at the stop!"

At the edge of the quay, a Senegalese wearing a *boubou*, squatting on his heels, tried to talk me into buying a small wooden giraffe. "My boy, my boy, come here, very cheap!" Masks, ivory, wooden sculptures, musical instruments thrown one on top of the other on a small blanket. Grandma Rose pulled me even harder, but she did promise, "You can come back with Henriette tomorrow." Did my aunt keep the promise her mother made? I can't remember.

Twenty metres away, the tram was ringing its bell; we broke into a run. This time, it was my turn to pull on Grandma's hand. "Shake a leg, lady, it's all aboard now!" His hat glued to his head, the motorman clapped his hands and enjoined us to hurry. "Up you go, up you go. Big step up! Good boy!"

The tram dropped us at the corner of Rue Endoume and Boulevard de la Corderie. Another ten-minute trot: Place

Joseph-Étienne, the steep slope of the Rue des Lices and then we're there – Rue Chaix.

Back in her own territory, Grandma Rose took the bit between her teeth and began galloping like a horse that smells its stable.

"Come on, Nico, just a bit further. Do you want me to take your bag?"

"No, Grandma, I can do it myself!"

At the bottom of the stairs, a creaking noise, and we looked up: a neighbour was hanging her wash out the window. The sky was a faded blue.

"Good evening, Rose. Good evening, *gàrri*."

"Good evening, Madame Rossi."

"How are you, Anna? We just got in from Moustiers."

And so on and so forth. As if we were returning from great travels. But the two minutes the conversation gave me to catch my breath at the foot of the stairs were welcome.

On the side of the hill topped by Notre-Dame-de-la-Garde, Rue Chaix (the inhabitants of the neighbourhood had called it *ru-ché* since time immemorial) ran about four hundred metres and had some sixty doors. It began at Rue des Lices and ended at Rue Vauvenargues, after describing a ninety-degree angle. Just before the elbow, about three-quarters of the way down the street, from number 26 to number 38, the street sloped steeply and boasted an abrupt set of steps, about one hundred in all. Grandma Rose and Henriette's house stood at number 36; ours, number 38, right at the top of the staircase.

Eugène and Virginie, Émile and Marie, and my four cousins lived at 42 and 42 *bis*, just past the steps, two small attached houses with a terrace and a little yard.

The staircase, though narrow, was split in two by a steel banister, on which the neighbourhood kids would wear out the seats of their pants. Gérard and I were no exception.

Come summertime, by nine o'clock, the steps would be full of neighbours sitting on the cool stone stairs. Every evening, assembled on the step closest to their respective doors, some twenty people would take the air and exchange the local gossip. A real working-class neighbourhood, a village within the city.

In front of number 36 was a landing of some twelve square metres before the last flight of steps. On it, two more doors: number 34 and in front, on the left side if you were going up, number 29, where a Spanish couple lived. Mr. and Mrs. Martinez had come to live in Marseille a few months after Francisco Franco y Bahamonde Salgado Prado entered Madrid on April 1, 1939. "*Este primero de Abril*, we decide we don't like the taste of the fish anymore," they used to say. I could understand their Iberian jabber better than most, though I never studied Castilian Spanish. And I can still belt out "*la niña, la niña-del fuego*" just like Señora Martinez – half-Andalusian, half-illusion, Jacques Brel would have said – who, without warning, would launch into song at irregular intervals during the day. I must have learned Spanish very young without even trying, thanks to Jesús Fernandez.

So many memories on that landing and those steps… I did not actually experience the one I remember with the most clarity: my grandmother told me about it once we arrived at her door, the very evening I left Moustiers.

Right in front of us, a huge hole, a good metre in circumference and at least thirty centimetres deep. Just beneath Aunt Henriette's bedroom window, in front of the cellar window. The cement still torn apart a good year later.

"And it took them three weeks to come and pick up the darn shell. You can imagine how afraid we were, sleeping right next to it…"

"What was the shell like, Grandma?"

"Like a shell! Lying on its side, black and pointed…"

"Was it big?"

"Big? Like a skipjack: at least a hundred kilos! But, thank God, it fell on its stomach."

This heavy artillery shell had landed on August 27, 1944, during the fight for the liberation of Marseille, while in Rose's cellar dug into the rock, a good fifteen neighbours and family members were packed like sardines. "Fortunately, it didn't blow. Or else, *peuchère*… The Holy Mother of Marseille saved us!"

And that was where, in that charmed place in Marseille, in the shadow of our merciful Protector, my father would recover the family that really wasn't his any more. But all the same, they would welcome him with open arms and make him feel as though he had always been one of them. And that was also where my father and I would be reunited.

❧ TWENTY ❧

Tuesday, June 12th. My father was supposed to arrive at the Saint-Charles station on one of the evening trains, but he hadn't been able to tell Uncle Eugène which one. At the time, rail transport was chaotic. The country was awakening and everyone wanted to go somewhere else, all at the same time. All the more so in what had been the Free Zone, where so many had come to take refuge in November of 1942, hoping to get to England or America or simply to avoid Nazi persecution. Numerous deportees were going home, of course, back to happy situations or nasty surprises. Uncle Émile, who managed to obtain a few litres of gas on the black market for his Citroën, took it upon himself to transport the welcoming committee made up of two brothers-in-law, Rose and me, of course. (I was wondering with some anxiety whether Uncle Émile would be able to drive the car with his eye in the shape it was in – black around it, red inside, almost closed!)

On the station platform, my grandmother kept tidying my hair, straightening my shirt, and giving me clear instructions:

"Don't forget to go forward and kiss him. And most of all, don't look surprised, even if you find him very thin…." Around us, the noise was staggering; the Aurelle, Forbin, and Audéoud barracks, as well as the Saint-Jean and Saint-Nicolas forts, had to open their doors for the hundreds of soldiers on leave who were arriving. Every exotic element of the French army seemed to be there on the platform: the *zouaves* with their curious baggy pants, Senegalese infantrymen with red *chéchias* on their black heads, Algerian units from the 7th RTA who had liberated Marseille, *spahis* from the great deserts draped in their capes, legionnaires with their white kepis… And sailors too, their berets topped with red pompons like the one in my father's picture, and white gaiters. A real Babel! A torrent of words poured forth on that platform, a thousand languages pattering, a thousand dialects and idioms meeting… But also, *pardi*, the sunlit tongue of the Midi – though it had difficulty being heard. A few steps away was a mischievous little girl; we communicated through signs and faces.

The first train arrived from Paris at 6:40 p.m. As it pulled up, the acrid odour of coal wafted through the station. Uncle Émile sat me on his shoulders ("But what's wrong with his eye, *boudiou*?") and I was the lookout: a lost cause, though, for my father wasn't on the train. Most of the passengers were deportees, that was easy to see: their faces were emaciated, their clothes much too big for their frail bodies. A few of them had kept their camp uniforms, the horrible striped outfit that they wore with a measure of pride. How I hoped Dad wouldn't be dressed like that! Cries, tears, hugs. All the confusion made the show slightly surreal.

I came down from my perch. Rose took my hand and gripped it tightly, my two uncles framing me. The little girl had disappeared.

The next train got in a good hour later, at 7:53 on the station's huge clock. Even before we could see it, a thundering noise announced its imminent arrival. An enormous plume of white smoke arose at the end of the platform; then, blurred by jets of vapour, the black locomotive appeared, slowly approaching. Once again, the acrid odour of coal. The noise of the crowd was so intense it made the train seem silent until it rolled to a stop with an endless squeal of brakes.

Perched on Uncle Émile's shoulders once more, I scanned the new arrivals in vain. My father spotted us first; we didn't notice him until he was a stone's throw away. For me, it was a terrible shock – he was so thin, so broken. The few seconds I needed to slip down to the ground was enough to hide my panic. He took me in his arms. "Do you remember me? You've changed, you know!" Not as much as him! Close up, his skin was even more wrinkled than Grandma's, and he seemed much older than his brothers-in-law, who were actually older than he was. At least he wasn't wearing that awful prisoner's garb. He had on a dark vest, rather becoming too, and a white shirt. A wide smile lit up his face. Immediately, I remembered that smile – it was the same as the one in the pictures. I felt all that in confused fashion: the image came from far away, from the furthest reaches of my childhood, like the faint light of a distant star...

Our embrace went on forever, with Eugène repeating, over and over, "Oh, brother! Oh, brother!" The expression has since become legendary in our family. My father interrupted them to ask about his wife's absence, which deflated our enthusiasm like a badly cooked *soufflé*. "Don't worry, Paul, she's well. She just sprained her ankle the day before yesterday," his mother-in-law lied. "Ah..." And in that extended "Ah," there was much to hear: the 'b' in bizarre, the 'c' in consternation, the 'd' in disappointment... all the way to the 's' in shit – a noble exclamation, a great consoler of human misery.

We made our way through the crowd. I insisted on being the one to carry our phantom father's luggage, and I held onto it proudly all the way to the car. It was very light: a tiny suitcase with only a few personal things.

A cardboard suitcase that, as he was leaving Dachau, he later told us, he had taken from one of those heaps of confiscated objects, since seen in more than one press photo – tragic monuments of concentration-camp art erected to memorialize the horror and savagery. In separate sculptures raised high, here were watches, there glasses or dentures, tufts of hair, handbags, shoes, belts, suitcases... Inside his, I would find clothes, papers, medication, perfume and a few knickknacks (including my first miniature Eiffel Tower) bought in Paris for a few pennies.

By the time we reached the Old Port, my father had tried several times to revive the conversation about my mother. But mum's the word! We preferred to let him rave on about the waterfront and on his right, the beautiful *Grand Siècle* city hall, so rich in memories for him, and on his left, Notre-Dame-de-la-Garde, perched on its hill, and the Saint-Victor abbey, leaning against the ramparts of Fort Saint-Nicolas – our neighbourhood. And then, with the tact and aplomb that she used to master difficult situations, Rose told him "what had changed." Dad's dry eyes found a way to secrete imperceptible tears that glinted with fleeting light. "Oh, I see…" And nothing more. Not a word. We respected his silence all the way to our destination, on Rue Chaix.

The apartment where I lived with my parents before the great family shake-up, at number 38 on that street, was right above the fully detached house at number 36, where Rose and Henriette lived. Our two windows gave onto their terrace, with a view all the way down to the port, the islands and the great sea beyond it. Home at last, my father sat down at one of the windows and looked out, like a sailor at his post. "But you'll come and have every meal with us," his mother-in-law added with that peremptory tone that she'd always match with surprising tenderness. Henriette echoed her mother's decision. "You'll always be welcome here, Paul. And your son will continue sleeping with us, in the third room." Good, wonderful Henriette, single her entire life, but a mother to all her nephews. My father, his heart adrift, quickly accepted this arrangement.

The day following his return, the whole family, with the notable exception of the three still in Moustiers, gathered together around a bowl of *pistou* on Rose and Henriette's veranda, which had lost all its windows during the battle to free the city in August 1944. Fit for a king, that *pistou* was full of nearly unobtainable ingredients – with a distinct aftertaste of overflowing emotion. It had been prepared, of course, by Aunt Virginie, under Eugène's attentive eyes, and was accompanied by two or three old bottles that he'd pulled from behind his woodpile. Disoriented and hurt, my father paid an exorbitant price for his first soup as a free man: a price worthy of Shylock, though he didn't have even a gram of flesh to pay with.

And my mother who was in such confusion a hundred kilometres away... And Gérard and Aunt Marie who must have been wondering too...

The meal lasted a good three hours. I remember that the accompanying conversation was often awkward, and lapsed into heavy silence more than once. But Eugène's wine was a good enough fuel. My father had been dry for a long time, and he needed only a glass to abandon his silence. He told several stories, and one has stuck with me since. Liberated from Dachau, he arrived at the Lutetia with a few other deportees, all in camp garb. They were led toward one of the hotel's grand salons, from which they could hear chamber music playing. As they entered the room, the musicians immediately stopped playing, stood up, saluted them, then began a loud rendition of the *Marseillaise*. My father confessed that his eyes had filled with tears.

Then he asked Uncle Émile what was behind the superb black eye he was sporting (I hadn't dared ask him). He admitted he'd fought with one of his harbour firefighter colleagues. When he announced that his brother-in-law was returning, the subtle fellow retorted that it couldn't have been that hard in the camps if my father had been able to survive!

Overall, the prisoners returning from Germany didn't receive a very warm welcome – people had gotten used to their absence. Of the four categories of prisoners, the volunteer workers and those of the "*Relève*"[8] got the worst reception – mostly contempt and hostility. The STO workers were not appreciated on their return either; everyone had a score to settle after the war, and people wondered why the STO guys couldn't have avoided service. Well, a lot of them did! Prisoners of war, by far the greatest number (almost a million men), did receive some consideration. But let's admit they hadn't made their country proud during the "Phoney War"! Though people were ready to commiserate with the skeletal deportees, they were rarely eager to listen to the litany of horrors they'd suffered – after all, in the homeland, everyone had paid. And then again, *basta*! It was time to forget the whole thing… Besides, how could they have put their suffering into words? And how could they have tolerated the shameless incredulity that often greeted them? Might as well keep quiet, swallow the bitter pill and silently suffer the terrible devastation within.

Sharp as can be, Henriette found the only possible remedy.

"Paul, the summer is terribly hot, and in the evening our terrace is cool enough. Invite your friends over to enjoy it!"

"But, Rose…"

"Don't be silly! This is your home, too. Come whenever you like, however many you may be. Every evening, if you wish."

★

A few days after my father's return, her shame swallowed, armed with unsteady courage, my mother came to see the man who was still her husband.

I remember they stayed at the far end of the terrace for a very long time, leaning on the railing. She must have told him, with great pain in her voice and tears streaming down her cheeks, that her decision was final. Perhaps she explained that, if she'd yielded to another man, it was only because she was in a time of complete distress, and she'd needed to survive her sadness. She must have encouraged him to take time to heal, to make an effort to pull himself together and maybe even to follow her example. Before she left, I saw her kiss him tenderly on the cheek. He lingered for a long while out on the terrace, alone.

How could I know what those two people, who had loved each other dearly and perhaps still did, felt at the time?

For whom was the ordeal most difficult? For my mother, who had to exact the unspeakable cruelty of her choice? For my father, who had to accept an implacable decision he could not change?

But in the end, when you return to life like Lazarus, and when you're not even forty... Since he had very few tears left and didn't want to ruin what life he had miraculously held onto, he took the chance he had and accepted the divorce without contesting it. Another woman, young and beautiful, would soon come into his life. Under the ashes of his misery, new happiness was brewing, waiting for him to seize it. After a cataclysm shatters your world, destroys your health, and reduces your home to ashes, you either give up on life or cling to it. Once more, my father stood tall – and took this new woman with open arms. He offered her his heart, and she did not refuse it. From then on, it would be another story, with its own joys and sorrows.

As for my own feelings, they were in a shambles... On one hand, a father I thought lost forever, who belonged to a past I was barely aware of, and in whose face I could not recognize the shining young sailor from the picture... On the other, Uncle Roger, a blessing from Heaven, source of happiness and contentment – he had reassured us, protected us, amused us and, best of all, healed my mother – and for all those reasons I saw him as one of the most wonderful people in my small world.

❧ TWENTY-ONE ❦

During my father's brief stay on Rue Chaix (he would live there from mid-June to the end of 1945), his comrades from the Resistance, who had happily accepted Henriette's invitation, would show up two or three times a week to enjoy the terrace and its cool air. There would always be five or six of them appearing in the straightening shadows of the evening, with Uncle Eugène often joining them later.

With the exception of Caraco, all of them – François, Joseph, Little Pierre, Raymond, Alexandre and Alfred – had, like my father, belonged to Doctor Gaston C.'s network. When I say all of them, I mean those who survived: those six and a few others, including Maguy Ducerf, Ange Casta, Georges Durand, and the doctor. Eleven survivors out of thirty-one.

Salutary moments of relaxation, of a few drinks and freedom as, together again, they slowly rose from their own ashes with the sumptuous nightly tableau of the port and the harbour slipping into darkness before them. They would meet to purge their minds of the painful memories that tortured them, exiling those memories with cathartic chatter that, strangely enough, would always be filled with humour.

They would break the bonds of their obsessive memories, and from their lips poured tales that transfixed me – the work Kommandos where comrades died of exhaustion under the blows of sadistic guards and bloodthirsty dogs, the roll calls in freezing German weather wearing only the lightest of clothes, the endless journeys in packed cattle cars, where the dead bodies of fallen comrades would be pushed into a corner to serve as a barrier to the piss and shit of the living... Sometimes, heroic stories would make me shudder, yet fill me with enthusiasm: the story of Caraco's cap, for example, or other feats they'd accomplished before their arrest. Like the story of François, he who was known as *Le Grava* (The Pockmarked).

Le Grava was the hottest of the hotheads in the network, and you can imagine that he wasn't afraid of anything. To say he feared nothing or no one would be putting it mildly. He'd always be charged with the most dangerous jobs and, once accomplished, he'd come back, salute and ask for more. He was something else, all right: unfailing courage, unbreakable determination. Before putting a bomb under a car, a knife through a heart, or even a bullet in someone's head, he first rehearsed everything, methodically, in his head. By the time he was ready for action, there was no hesitation or doubt; the execution of the act was a mere formality. And when someone would congratulate him for his courage and audacity, he answered with a modest shrug, quoting Corneille: "To conquer without danger is to triumph without glory!" He might not have been the best student, but he had learned that line by heart.

In early 1943, the Wehrmacht, which had occupied the South of France since the November 11, 1942, hardened their line under the direction of the ubiquitous Gestapo. François *Le Grava* was given the mission to eliminate the SS colonel responsible for the execution of several Resistance fighters, shot in the courtyard of the Saint-Nicolas fort in Marseille. "I'm going skin him quick, the bastard!" The colonel had his quarters in a posh building on the Cours Pierre-Puget, occupying the three floors with his bodyguards, maids and servants – fifteen people in all. *Le Grava* quickly gathered enough information for his dangerous mission. Our man slipped into the building early one morning with the help of a coal delivery man. He hid in the basement, behind a boiler and a pile of coal. The cubbyhole was small and dark, and he had to stay there until nightfall, crouched in his hideout, careful and attentive to every sound: distant voices, a shouted order, a door slamming, soldiers climbing up and down the stairs… A soldier in darkness, he waited patiently for his moment, refusing to think too much. There was no point in it: he knew how, with a short, skilful movement, to slice through the carotid or slip a blade under the diaphragm to reach the heart or a major artery. He was gifted in the matter.

After several long hours, all sounds abated. *Le Grava* could finally stretch his sore limbs and get his strength back with some limbering exercises. A confident professional, he was in no hurry. He waited another half-hour – his indispensable margin of security.

He knew exactly where on the second floor the colonel was sleeping. He also knew that the room next door was bristling with armed guards. But he wasn't worried.

No sound could be heard. He emerged from his hiding place and climbed the stairs, each floor bathed in the soft glow from a skylight. He climbed patiently, making sure no floorboards creaked; a cat couldn't have been quieter. He reached the colonel's door, tried to open it – locked! He took out a master key, jigged the lock a little, and it yielded without a sound. Phew! No inside lock. The door opened onto complete darkness. He entered and closed the door behind him, walked a few steps and stopped… His eyes quickly grew used to the darkness, and now he made out a tiny night light floating in a glass bulb, sitting on a piece of furniture – the colonel's bedside table. He moved forward. On the table, an automatic pistol. He pocketed it and took out his tool: a small Corsican *vendetta* whose blade was as sharp as a razor. The night light's flickering flame glinted off its tip. A knife held with a firm hand, the hand of a throat-slitter and a strangler – war, like *noblesse*, obliges. Next to him, peacefully sleeping, the colonel savoured his last night on this earth. An excellent idea, this night light: the filth will be the spectator of his own demise… It's done often enough in the Gestapo!

At the bedside of the condemned, *Le Grava* woke him by pushing his hand over his mouth and his blade before his eyes.

Horrified, supplicating eyes, as wide as saucers. With a quick twist of his wrist, *Le Grava* slit his throat, with a smile as big as the open wound. A good hand, precise, quick, strong: it never betrayed him. A pious hand, too, from time to time: with a sign of the cross, it absolved the man it just dispatched to another world, offering with that devout gesture an *Ausweis* for a trip without return. "Always respect the death of another man, whoever he might be!" That was the pious François's motto.

The network's last mission, two days before the May 25, 1943, arrests, was entrusted to Raymond, who had volunteered to eliminate the militiaman responsible for Armand's arrest – the first among many who'd soon be in the hands of the enemy, taken on the 17th as he was leaving his office. Mercier was the name of the militiaman, a Frenchman to boot!

Insults, humiliation, fists to the face and kicks to the belly: then covered in his own blood, the poor comrade was thrown into the Militia's vehicle.

Raymond took up position near the restaurant, on Rue Beauvau, where Mercier often ate his midday meal. The traitor arrived, followed by two henchmen. They walked past him without noticing Raymond, whose nose was stuck in the newspaper he was holding. His bike stood against the wall.

That was Raymond, whom my father said had a heart "big like this," with a generous expanse of his hands. That was true enough. He never backed down, never abandoned, never gave up, even under punishment and threats.

The wait was endless. Then the three men came out. They passed right in front of Raymond without looking at him. He leaped up and stuck a knife in Mercier's side. The traitor stopped in his tracks and fell to his knees. Raymond jumped on his bike and turned the corner quickly enough to avoid the bullets.

A passerby who was, by chance, on the other side of the street (it was Little Pierre waiting for the results) informed him that same night of his mission's success.

I also heard on my grandmother's terrace, with the moonlight shining down, another expert in expedited solutions tell a few stories of his own: Joseph the *Goï* – the same one who had escaped the arrests at the doctor's headquarters.

All alone, but keeping in mind his leader's instructions, he continued for a time with direct and delaying action before offering his services to a cell in the Var region. "It's our duty to keep the Occupation army in a constant state of insecurity, to wage a war of attrition, to push it to react violently and alienate the population – a population of indifferent and passive citizens that will have to wake up at some point, for Christ's sake! Can't make an omelette without breaking eggs, boys."

A fisherman by trade, Jo decided one day to take down a battery situated in one of the blockhouses built on the Corniche promenade. He calmly rowed his way up to a blockhouse, no problem, and then it was easy enough just to toss in a grenade and – *boom!* Right in the middle of the gunners who'd neglected to wave as he passed. "You have to admit, they deserved a lesson in manners!" he joked. His one regret? He wasn't able to use the same trick twice. After his exploit, the gunners in the coastal batteries welcomed any approaching craft with a salvo of gunfire. "Just plain impolite, don't you think?"

Another time, he'd blown up a German vedette boat. He was placing his lines near the Planier lighthouse when the vedette slowly came about. On board, three men wearing the Kriegsmarine's white uniform, with that strange little black hat and its slightly feminine ribbons. At least these ones were polite, even courteous. They addressed him in a friendly manner, and he vaguely understood they were asking if the fish were biting. Smiling, he bent down into his boat, as if looking for a nice catch to show off… Instead, he came back with a live grenade. The detonation almost sent him to the bottom with his victims. "Without a doubt, the hardest thing I'd done – those three affable faces, looking at me without suspicion… They often haunt my dreams, I'll tell you…"

Needs must when the devil drives… But what horror, what stupidity!

And so, on the terrace, I would shudder with fear late into the night when the conversation would turn to these matters. I would sit still and drink in every word they spoke until – always much too early – Grandma would come outside, wearing a smile but with a tone that left me no options. "Dominique, it's time to go to bed. Say goodnight to your Dad and these gentlemen."

❧ TWENTY-TWO ❧

Maguy, Ange, Georges, and the Doctor never came to the evenings on Rue Chaix. Back from the camps, the first three went home: Maguy to Aix-en-Provence, Georges to Sainte-Tulle, near Manosque, and Ange to Bonifacio. I never met Georges, who killed himself shortly after his return, and I met Maguy and Ange the day of Raymond's funeral.

In the early fifties, my father introduced me to the doctor and his wife during one of the frequent visits he made to their house on the Cours Devilliers, where their network had been broken up in 1943 and where the doctor still had his practice. I was a student at the Lycée Thiers at the time, only ten minutes away. I would soon come to know the place very well, since the couple, who had no family of their own and was rather withdrawn from the world, expressed the desire to see me again. They were so kind to me – they welcomed me as if I were a nephew – that my visits soon became weekly.

In the living room where we would sit, in plain sight on a console table, I noticed the picture of a young man with a broad smile: their only son Christian, who died in a camp in the last few weeks of the war. He'd also been a member of his father's network. The ultimate sacrifice for his country at twenty-three years old. In front of the picture, under a glass pane that also held a tri-coloured ribbon in the upper left corner, a hand-written page read:

March 14, 1945, do you remember? We were evacuated from Vaihingen. Despite our protests, we weren't allowed in the same car. Unknown destination. Two days later, Dachau. I rushed to your car. You were among the dead they were throwing onto the platform. They beat me, set a dog on me, they stopped me from getting near you, from taking you in my arms. But since that day, you haven't left me, and I haven't left you.

Papa

On the far side of the living room was a bookcase, a large piece of furniture with panes of glass. Half the space was reserved for scientific works and the other half for literary ones.

The first thing I noticed about the room was its particular odour, which I can still smell today, but that I couldn't describe except to say it was slightly sweet. The odour probably emanated from the books, since it always seemed more present when we opened the bookcase doors.

I spent long hours in that room, choosing the books I'd borrow for the week. Sometimes, when his schedule permitted, the doctor would come and see me between two patients to guide me in my choice or gather my impressions of the most recently read work. He especially enjoyed Pierre Loti and Anatole France, the latter for his anticlerical views and social ideas – two authors who were never mentioned in school. He recommended that I begin my education with *The Crime of Sylvestre Bonnard*. He said nothing more. I was surprised to find not even a trace of a crime plot, yet I was certainly not disappointed. This subtle story, "written in the shadow of other books," would reveal itself to be an excellent introduction. I soon devoured an entire shelf full of Anatole France's best titles and a few of Pierre Loti's exotic travel books that took me from the Basque country to Bretagne and Iceland, via Greece, Turkey and Japan. That first year, Madame C. suggested that I read Jean Giono's *Pan Trilogy* – *Hill of Destiny, Lovers Are Never Losers,* and *Harvest,* which brought me straight back to the heart of my dear Provence and reminded me – with great melancholy – of the Moustiers of my childhood, the setting of my first emotions.

In early 1953, a few days after my sixteenth birthday, the doctor's wife invited me for a flute of champagne. There would be a guest, I was told, a long-standing friend they wanted me to meet.

I arrived on time on a Sunday afternoon and was welcomed into the living room. Their guest, a man in his sixties with a pleasant face and mischievous eyes, put down his pipe and offered me his hand. "I hear, young man, that you're interested in literature..." It was Jean Giono, in the flesh. Madame C. brought out a cake she'd prepared for the occasion, the doctor opened a bottle of champagne and the discussion quickly warmed. At first I was shy, but I quickly felt at ease with this charming trio. I stopped thinking I was taking an exam or giving an oral presentation and began to respond spontaneously to the questions asked, even revealing my own doubts and questions. An unforgettable lesson about the authenticity of reading and the true pleasure I could take from it. I won't soon forget that afternoon.

Giono, so true to himself, whose pacifist writings in the thirties offended the warlike France of 1939 and even more so the revanchist France and the numerous overnight Resistance fighters of 1944 – his pen would twice earn him a stay in jail. But the sincerity and humanity of the writer (whose complete pacifism was no comfort, far from it) was appreciated by the dear doctor, who never mistook his childhood friend for Brasillach, Drieu la Rochelle, or any of their consorts, those abhorrent and misguided authors.

★

Dany, my former schoolmate whom I'd seen only once or twice over the years and saw again in Moustiers in April of 1953, was also impressed.

"You saw Jean Giono?"

"As clearly as I see you! We even had a long conversation."

I knew how to take advantage of the situation. I spoke at length and with great authority of the *Pan Trilogy*. I had devoured those novels with such an appetite!

How the young woman had filled out the promises of the girl; she had turned into a very pretty thing indeed! Our relationship developed rather quickly. Our year-and-a-day age difference didn't matter any more. What she had acquired in chest size, I had in height, and I was now a good head taller than she. She accepted the idea of a little moon-lit walk to the edge of the village; it was already quite warm in Prov-ence at the end of April. "But I need to be home before midnight."

Were I to believe her, she was most impressed by the change in the size of my shoulders.

"I do a lot of sports at school – gymnastics, the high jump, running, handball."

"I mostly dance."

"I can see that by the shape of your legs."

"You think they're too big?"

"Not at all. They're muscular and wonderfully shaped. Your calves are… exquisite. As for your thighs, I can't tell yet."

Just like that, I made my request. And since we were non-chalantly lying in the grass, it was instantly satisfied.

Our youthful enthusiasm quickly exhausted us, and I re-member how hard it was not to fall asleep with her. Without the village clock tower… But twelve tolls of the bell are usu-ally enough to wake the dead. In the end, Dany's lateness went unnoticed. Our short night would never be repeated, and I would only have an encore in my memories.

In July, the proud young woman would return to Moustiers with a diploma, having scored high on all her exams. I was already in the village, having insisted on spending the first few weeks of my vacation there. Émile and Marie were always happy to welcome their nephews. "The rooms upstairs are there for a reason."

As soon as I got her alone *souto li pin*, I complimented, per-haps with too much enthusiasm, the girl I called, with great naiveté, "my Dany." But, quickly enough, I had to come to terms with the disagreeable facts: her heart was no longer in it and her mind, no doubt occupied with more important ven-tures than me, forbade her body to waste energy on a now-futile endeavour. And so life goes.

This misadventure remained a sore spot for me, but at least it allowed me to write a liberating poem that, once finished, I decided not to share with my innocent torturer. Since then, nostalgically, I've kept it for my eyes only.

> *Our love first bloomed in early summer*
> *And our hearts lost their cold pallor*
> *As we lay under the budding moon,*
> *And for each other sang and swooned.*
>
> *Thy skin is white like mother's milk*
> *And from your fountainhead I wish to drink*

So I lay my mouth on yours, but my heart doest sink
Knowing you'll refuse me your silk

Oh, why doest the buds of May bloom?
For into leaves they'll turn soon
And then they fall in winter's shadow
And will be left in the dead meadow

Where we used to sit and talk of love
Before your heart – fickle dove –
Left it for another spring
And now I must tend my broken wings.

❧ TWENTY-THREE ❦

Evening come, as day turned into night, we often cried on the terrace – tears of laughter, more often than not. The stories weren't all funny, far from it, but they very rarely finished on a sad note. The funniest one was Little Pierre's.

In 1943, the year of his arrest, Little Pierre was twenty-three years old and engaged – well, not exactly, but almost. In his mind, in any case, he was married, and also in the imagination of his sweetheart, Mathilde de Saint-Onge, whom he'd met in October of the previous year, at the start of the new semester at the Faculty of Letters in Aix-en-Provence. By Easter, probably by Palm Sunday, they were already speaking of marriage. She loves him, of course she loves him. With every fibre of her little heart. Does it not beat with fervour every time she sees him? Me too, my love, I could never live without you. Why hesitate, let's get married – next year, next month! Spirits run high under the burning Provençal sun.

But to make those words a reality… The fact was that Mathilde's parents hadn't exactly warmed to Pierre on his first visit to the family home. They lived in a posh house on the heights above Marseille, in Roucas-Blanc, from which one could gaze at the endless sea. And since, on the second visit, they had been no more enthusiastic – smiles are not always signs of cordiality – Pierre understandably decided that there would be no third meeting in the near future.

As for the Saint-Onge family, they were ship chandlers, from one generation to the next, since the nineteenth century. Following the well-known snowball principle, Mathilde's father, the most recent of the line, didn't even know how rich he was. It was very clear to Pierre's eyes since, after all, he did use them for seeing, that the tragic situation in France under the heel of the German boot had not affected the well-to-do family's sumptuous circumstances. (As proof, a small Pissaro and two large Degas paintings hung on the wall of their living room – bought at a steal, the sanctimonious Mathilde explained, from their neighbours, two nice Jews who'd suddenly deserted Marseille without leaving so much as an address…)

"The second time I went to their home, it was for some kind of function. I had no desire to go, but Mathilde insisted. So I put on whatever looked best in my closet – meaning the cheap suit I'd bought a month earlier for my thesis defence (I'd just finished my master's on Pirandello's theatre) – and I ignored my bitterness to please my dear Mathilde. I never change, eh? I get to the place all prettied up and as soon as I walk through the door, I feel like an idiot: I'm certainly not dressed for the occasion. Mathilde's look made that clear enough… Just imagine: among the guests there were several

Kraut officers, not to mention some of the region's *Pétainiste* debris!"

Pierre's father, Monsieur Scotto, was unfortunately not related to Vincent Scotto, the creator of the Marseille operetta and the author of several hundred songs, including some very famous ones, like *La Petite Tonkinoise* and *J'ai deux amours*. As for Marcel Scotto, he was a simple mason – and a labourer to boot, not a boss. Besides, since those fateful visits, Pierre, who was no fool, was starting to have serious doubts about the possibility of marriage to a girl whom, as a sensible boy, he no longer saw in the same light. Hadn't he observed that Mathilde's opposition to her parents was no longer as strong? That she was becoming less spontaneous with him, that she looked at him differently? No doubt it's difficult to disagree with your mother and father, especially when they're indecently rich. No easier than to throw yourself, without a penny, into a marriage with a rich heiress whose intentions seem to be faltering.

The forced separation of the spring of 1943 had at least one advantage: Pierre's passion cooled and he began to open his eyes. The whole thing was quite a banal business, a vaudeville sketch, really, but hurtful all the same. He had all the time he needed in the camps, where unhappiness took on a whole new dimension, to mull over the experience and turn it to ridicule. The treatment was most effective and Pierre quickly came to the conclusion that Mathilde wasn't for him.

In the camps, occasions to laugh were so few and far between that there was no chance he'd let that one go! He started to tell his tragic love story more and more frequently, adding details here, removing others there, asking for his friends' opinions and then their participation. The story slowly grew, and soon enough it had turned into a sketch they all enjoyed acting out, each interpreting a character in the story in their own way. The actual plot was rather thin and repetitive, so they took to concentrating on its details, blowing them out of proportion. Little Pierre was convincing as the lovelorn, broken-hearted lover; other times he played the young, frustrated fiancé starting to show signs of exasperation. Caraco was excellent as the father, Monsieur de Saint-Onge in the flesh. He was the oldest of the bunch, but also the only one able to speak convincingly of hunting dogs and the Poitou marshes where he'd run them, a place he had never set foot in. He also liked to play an SS colonel close to the family, and he brought his role to new heights by making a monocle with a bit of wire. His modest prop would let him quickly switch from Monsieur de Saint-Onge to Colonel Friedrich Krupp von Bohlen – "the magnate of the Ruhr steel mills," he'd always add.

All this to say that the show was well rehearsed by the time they staged it at 36 Rue Chaix. Little Pierre or somebody else (I'd often ask for it) would propose we play "The Pleasures of Love" (the title came from Grandma Rose, who'd often hum the well-known tune), and then it would be all hands on deck!

In a minute, the chairs were carried onto the veranda and set in a row, backs to the sea, for the lighting on the terrace where we usually met was woefully insufficient, even on full-moon nights. This set-up allowed us to create a space of some ten metres between the spectators and the veranda, which would become our stage, lit by the harsh white light of the wall lamp between the kitchen and the dining room's French doors. Too bad about the mosquitoes that, no doubt having heard how it was done at Pearl Harbour, attacked us in waves like kamikazes, risking their lives. The slap of our hands against our arms and legs rarely coincided with the actors' lines. But what can you do? The show must go on!

The curtain rises. Little Pierre, back to the light, taps his pipe three times against the terrace rail. Silence falls. "As you can see, we are in the magnificent living room of the great Saint-Onge family [his hand sweeps across the expanse of the now-materialized living room], where we meet…" He puts a capital letter on each name he calls out and, one after the other, the characters rise from their chairs, step on stage, and bow to the audience in the orchestra pit. "And now, let us see what we shall see!" Pierre sits down, but he'll be back soon enough to play his own role or maybe Mathilde's – a few effeminate gestures to straighten a lock of hair or send a greeting to someone will be more than enough to convince the audience that he is the passionate lovebird about to fly away.

My father played Firmin, the major-domo, since no one could open a bottle of champagne and serve the guests as stylishly as he could, his left hand behind his back. Caraco, wearing a new "Made in France" monocle, gave his performance more complexity by playing both his roles simultaneously, performing a rapid-fire dialogue between his two characters; he was just as quick as the great Chaplin himself. Once, in the middle of this hilarious scene, Rose had to run to the bathroom, and everyone understood why.

From time to time, when *Le Grava*, who usually played the role, was absent, Little Pierre transformed himself into the excessively sinuous and voluptuous Madame de Saint-Onge, making desperate efforts to replicate her husband's aristocratic poses, for he, unlike her, did not have common blood. Jo, whose limp had saved him from the camps, found a way to join the company by using his infirmity. He was Monsieur de la Grated Apple, a close neighbour who had had an unfortunate fall from his horse while riding somewhere in the Périgord region on his father-in-law's estate. Sometimes, following his inspiration, he became Monsieur de la Melted Tower, another neighbour from Roucas who had tumbled, during a night of drinking, down the great staircase in his manor (a place that had even more windows than the Saint-Onge home). Yet the two roles were almost identical: essentially, he'd refuse Firmin's champagne, exclaiming, "No! Bring me port wine, for Heaven's sake, a twenty-year-old vintage and nothing else!" Then he would stuff his face full of canapés, making good use of the large mouth he'd inherited from his father, a distant cousin of Fernandel, and which would execute hilarious masticating effects. To top it all off, on certain nights, his chimerical canapés would take on a more-than-real appearance as a plate of Henriette's fluffy, golden *oreillettes*!

As for me, as soon as the show's preparations would begin, I'd abandon the fig or the chocolate square I was nibbling on (in Marseille, it had a distinctively American flavour), run to grab Grandma, Auntie, and sometimes even Eugène in the neighbouring house if he wasn't on the terrace already. He soon joined the company too, proposing a most unexpected character: a grotesque collaborator, a sort of Troll under the Bridge based on Moretti whom, of course, he played to perfection the very first time, with a Raimu accent. A true actor, that Eugène!

The show would inevitably end with an overlaid scene that reminded the troupe of the cruel reality of the concentration camps, but that scene served only to turn it to ridicule and make it as funny as a spoonful of soup greedily gulped down, funny faces and all, his nose in the bowl – Raymond's specialty.

Raymond, a gangly fellow made of all bones and a profile like a bird of prey, had returned from the camps with his bronchus eroded by tuberculosis and had recently undergone an induced pneumothorax. Raymond was very nice to me, and I had great affection for him. I was always anxious when he joined the show. We had to be careful with him, since the slightest effort had him gasping for breath and he had difficulty finishing his sentences. The winks he bestowed to reassure me only pained me further; I couldn't smile and act as if nothing was wrong.

It was quite a spectacle, our outdoor theatre, with its natural backdrop of night sky studded with stars. And its treats, desserts, and tisanes were as warm as the bottom of our hearts. At times, the heavy blast of a steamship horn would travel all the way to our ears, through the dark and the distance.

৵ TWENTY-FOUR ৎ

"That I'm still breathing today is a real miracle. Without my friends around me, I'd have never made it through."

They would all say the same. After days and nights of watching death take their closest neighbours, after living for months and months among stiff corpses, smelling their pestilential odour, they knew, beyond all official statistics, that they were the true survivors of concentration camps and among a tiny minority who had made their way back from Hell. Coming from them, the word "miracle" was no exaggeration. Solidarity had united them. Friendship had been their ultimate bulwark against the Nazi machine's constant violence, a violence that had ground millions to dust. And the true miracle was that their trifling defence had resisted savage and systematic oppression. Yet it can be easily explained: the body, even worn out, crumbles only if the spirit fails. Against the enormous enterprise of humiliation, demoralization, and dehumanization that was the concentration camps, solidarity and friendship alone were able to provide them the strength to fight on, to refuse to collapse into obedience and resignation. In the camps, to bend was to break.

At Rose and Henriette's, Fred related, "I was at the end of my rope that day, a real wreck. I'd gotten it hard that morning, in the quarry. And we were putting on the play that night in our Block."

The others, who also remembered, took their places on the terrace.

"Come on, Fred. We need an SS officer. Not tonight, Pierre, I'm hurting."

"And I let them put on their play without me, broken and in pain."

Pierre called out to no one in particular, "Today... A Grand Ball at the Saint-Onge Palace!"

Caraco, facing the orchestra, his conductor's baton at the ready. On his signal, Alexandre, the violinist, begins to play energetically: *Jealousy...* Raymond, on the bandoneon, adds the frills and trills.

Fred continued his story. The Kraut insulted him and beat him. A rain of punches. The stomach, the chest, the face. Blood poured out of him.

Jealousy... François takes Pierre by the hand. Slowly, ceremonially, he brings him to the middle of the ballroom. François dances lasciviously with Mathilde. He's rather tall, and Pierre rather short – an odd tango. And both are so thin, a *danse macabre* with tango steps.

Then came the feet, Fred explained. Crumpled on the ground, the kicks came from all sides. Moans, cries of pain. But never a complaint, ever!

The dancers take great strides. From time to time, with his left hand, Mathilde adjusts her hair. A vigorous step and then, pivoting, a brutal stop: the dance is done. The couple salutes, everyone claps. Not Fred, impossible.

Alexandre settles in at the piano. In front of the imaginary keyboard, measured with a glance, he loudly cracks his knuckles. Pauses for inspiration, forehead lowered, gathering the notes in his head. Suddenly, he sets them free with great gestures, fingers splayed. Two minutes of intense gesticulation, then his last powerful chord. Motionless on his bench, eyes on the keys. He gets up and takes a bow.

"I was bad off, and my friends noticed. They finished the show and started fussing over me. Pierre came back with a half-bowl of soup. 'Drink it, Fred.' 'No, thanks. It won't go down.' 'Make an effort, for Heaven's sake. Such good soup… it's *pistou*! Paul made it for you.'"

So he drank it and soon felt better. They were the Musketeers: "All for one and one for all!" There was no other way.

★

From the Fresnes prison, my father was sent to Germany with some very heavy baggage – a death sentence and two letters that would open the gates of hell for him.

On December 7, 1941, Hitler published the *Nacht und Nebel* ("Night and Fog") directive according to which inhabitants of occupied territories who had been arrested for "terrorist activities" were to disappear into "night and fog" – the poetic wording that designated the concentration camps. The orders of Reichsführer Himmler, who'd been given the responsibility of implementing the directive, were as clear as day: "The Führer is of the opinion that in such cases, penal servitude or even a hard labour sentence for life will be regarded as a sign of weakness. An effective and lasting deterrent can be achieved only by the death penalty or by taking measures that will leave the family and the population uncertain as to the fate of the offender. Deportation to Germany serves this purpose." From then on, the so-called terrorists would be sent to Germany to die in secret.

In November 1943, my father was interned in the Neue Bremm camp as an NN. My mother was officially informed of his false disappearance. In our family's case, a lowly bureaucrat, more expeditious than his superiors, must have preferred the destruction of hope to the sadistic uncertainty of the directive.

⮞ TWENTY-FIVE ⮜

The guys had just sat down and hadn't yet picked up the conversation. They first had to catch their breath after their long climb up the steep stairs. Their furtive contemplation of the sea and the islands, warmed by the last rays of sun, had lessened their anxieties. They began feeling the enveloping tenderness of their unbreakable friendship – a friendship once wrought in the heart of the deepest pain, each day shared.

Rose and Henriette took out the usual sweets. Fruits mostly, which came from the *pòti* that Rose made with Rachel and Eugène, her neighbours from the Place Joseph-Étienne. And a few figs from the garden, since it was summer.

In the narrow yard that ran under the terrace and all the way to the edge of the cliff, ending in a point like a boat's bow, there were three fig trees. Each one was different from the others. The first, hanging onto the small wall that separated our garden from that of our immediate neighbours, the Devaux, drew glory from being the earliest. Always a good fifteen days ahead of the other two, its Marseille figs (also called *blanquettes* or Athens figs) of a light-green shade, almost white, opened to reveal flesh the colour of beef blood, dotted with yellow. They were fleshy and sweet but without excess sugar and only mildly flavoured. The second tree, the tallest, had imperiously grown in the middle of the bow that it now shaded with its thick foliage. It would give violet figs with a blue sheen and red-orange flesh – Black Bourjassottes, they were called. They were prettier than the Marseille variety and better too, with a heartier taste. And we always had more of them, since their maturation would last into late October. The third, a simple *figuieireto*, was less than two metres high and had pushed out of the ground under the tall tree's shadow. A bastard, no doubt, an unrecognizable species. The last to give us fruit, and never before mid-September, it produced small blackish figs, stunted and as wrinkled as an incubator baby's behind. But when it came to taste, those figs won the grand prize! "Candied!" Rose would say. That was the word for them. They melted in your mouth, "making your taste buds dance," Eugène the connoisseur would add, as much an expert on figs as on *pistou*. "The fig is Provence's most generous fruit. When she is ripe, she lets you know by dropping a small pearl of syrup from her operculum, that little eye there, under her belly. And she embodies the three cardinal virtues: humility – she bows her head; poverty – her gown is torn; and contrition – she has a tear in her eye. She is also our most religious fruit," concluded our miscreant, who never set foot in church. But *aco's de figo d'un autre panie*: that's another story.

Of all the wonderful fruits, the ones I preferred were the small dried bananas that my father sometimes brought back from downtown. They were brown, as if caramelized, and had a slightly elastic consistency. A discovery. And they were sticky, adding to the pleasure of being able to suck your fingers meticulously so as to not lose a single morsel. Better than chocolate!

Of course, there were also – but certainly not often enough, since the ingredients were hard to find – Henriette's *oreillettes*, which Grandma would always herald with a great "And now, sirs, the *oreillettes*, fashioned by the beautiful Henriette's nimble fingers!" That would always make my shy aunt blush. Especially when Caraco was there, his eyes full of desire.

They could have married, those two. She went to vespers at Notre-Dame-de-la-Garde almost every Sunday. Yet it was not to be…

That night, *Le Grava* arrived late. Completely red in the face, he shouted like Ruy Blas with an artillery man's voice, "*Bon appétit*, boys!" His words held no bitterness; they were exploding with joy. "I've got good news, boys! My pal Jean from General Intelligence just told me they're on the trail of one of our good friends. Guess who? Bet you'll never guess…" A long silence. We were all trying to figure it out.

"Tortora!"

"Tortora? Our very own Tortora from Rue Paradis?"

"In the flesh. After breaking plenty of our guys, including you and me, and living the high life during the Occupation, he disappeared incognito and went to cultivate his garden in a village in the Ardèche, near Aubenas."

"Are you sure?"

"Almost. Jean told me he'd pursue the search and keep me informed."

"I hope you'll keep an eye on him."

"Don't worry, Paulo. I'll be in Jean's office every day of the week."

"And then?"

"Then? As soon as I have the address of that scavenger, I'll go offer him last rites."

I can still see his eyes: like those of a child who's been promised a visit to the circus next Thursday – and those of a caged lion that sees his lunch arriving.

"Don't you think the time for forgiveness…"

"Quit your sermons, Caraco! You never met the Marseille Gestapo…"

"It's true Ludo, *Grav* is right. Tortora was despicable. Other people's suffering gave him a hard-on. And if he's still alive, we have to—"

"Kill him. That's that."

"No. Hatred, the more I think of it, the more…"

"You think too much."

Then *Le Grava* explained that it wasn't hate; it was just punishment – a big difference.

"Are you sure there's no hate in your heart?"

"Yes. The horrors that rotten Frenchman committed…"

Those horrors demanded that he be executed. For all the suffering he inflicted, for all those who died because of him. An eye for an eye. That's how humanity is, what can you do…

"I'll go with you, *Grav.*"

"Me, too!"

"No thanks, boys… you know I prefer to work alone. But don't worry, I'll have a little chat with him first. I'll pass on your greetings and remind him of his favourite game."

"The triangular ruler!"

"Exactly."

"What kind of ruler is that, *Papa?*"

Tortora didn't use it to draw. How could he have drawn with those fat sausage fingers that kept him from any delicate work? Probably remembering elementary school, where his performance must have been modest, he held onto his small triangular aluminum ruler. Now an adult, he used it in a very personal manner. Hitting the prisoners' fingers? Much too ordinary! His game consisted in putting it on the floor, in front of his victims, and forcing them to kneel on it. Then he jumped on their backs and threw himself into a gallop. "Giddy-up, girl, giddy-up!" Jumping up and down: guaranteed pain and humiliation. That's how he smashed my father's knee. The injury gave him terrible pain in the camps, and it never fully healed.

★

That same night (Was it really? No matter), Little Pierre was all smiles. All afternoon, he'd been trying to find Mathilde. Just to tell her he was still alive, nothing else. Yet he couldn't find her anywhere, not a trace, but what he'd discovered made him happy. The store her father owned on the Rive-Neuve Quay had just been sold and their sumptuous property in Roucas-Blanc was empty. The very popular purification had reversed the roles: it was now the biters' turn to be bitten. Delighted at having had the presence of mind to extract himself from the situation he'd been in, Pierre was in high spirits, and we were treated to a lengthy scene between Jo and him – a sort of half-fiction story about how, after having come close to being caught in an SS ambush, he'd been picked up for certain of his writings. As for Jo, he told the story of how he managed to slip through their nets.

Little Pierre had been caught with the others at the doctor's house on May 25, 1943. "All of them driven off in a covered truck. As you know, I was watching it from the Azur Hôtel," Jo recalled.

Then, at a street corner, thanks to a turn taken too tightly that shook the truck carrying the prisoners to their fate, Little Pierre, the last one to be brought to the truck, pushed the soldiers on either side of him and leaped for freedom – or death. Three or four gunshots; the bullets didn't hit him. A side street. He ran for it, he was free!

"So I go straight to my house and explain the situation to my parents. I take everything that might be compromising – not much, in any case. My revolver, my address book (all in code, of course), a few drafts of some pamphlets I'd been told to write up. Then I make my way to the house of some good friends who live on the other side of our street. I spend the night there. The next morning, around seven, as I'm getting ready to go back to my place to grab a change of clothes, from the window of the room where I spent the night, I see a black front-wheel drive stop in front of my house. Three men get out: special-section militiamen. They ring at the door. It opens. They enter. They come back ten minutes later without my parents – thank Heaven. The hours pass, and I'm still afraid to leave my hideout. Then I decide to leave early in the after-noon, after thanking my hosts, because I don't want to expose them any more than I already had. Two minutes with my parents, then I go seek refuge at a friend's house, a guy I met in university who lives on the Corniche promenade, facing the monument to the Army of the Orient, about fifteen minutes away. He's at home and agrees to shelter me. A good guy. I stay four days there, and then I go to Jo's, who wasn't there the night of the arrests. I take the Pointe-Rouge train to reach your house. Your wife tells me that she hasn't seen you since the 25th and that she has no idea of where you might be."

"Michelle was careful. She didn't even trust you. I'd told her so often to never trust anyone…"

"Of course. But she does tell me she'll try to find out more information. I understand and don't push the matter. She gives me one of your caps and some fisherman's equipment – a rod, line, hooks, a knife. Fifteen minutes later, I'm posted on a rock where she asked me to wait. I grab a couple of mussels and become an amateur fisherman! Two hours go by, and the funniest thing is that they're really biting! Labrum, rainbow wrasse, bream, stripped bass – at least a kilo of rock fish, enough to make a great soup!"

"The meek shall inherit the earth."

"You can say that again, *Grav*!"

"And then I show up."

"Yup. I see you in your double-ender. I jump in and we embrace."

"Of course. I saw you go into that German truck, and I knew nothing about what happened next."

"We tell each other the two sides of the same story – your luck in front of the doctor's house and my *salto mortale*. Then you give me the chance to hide with you in your cabin in Goudes."

"I'd been hiding out there for two nights already. I spent the night of May 25th in the hotel, and the next two nights at Eugène's. I still remember Virginie's delicious pasta."

"Sure, with only two tomatoes and a whisker of cheese…"

"In the boat," Little Pierre went on, "we talked, we tried to figure out what to do next… Maybe we could contact another network."

"But what did we know about the rest of the organization? Nothing, or next to nothing. No one left to link up with: how could we continue the fight?"

"Personally, I had my idea: a friend on the railroad, a militant communist who participated actively in railway sabotage. I talked to you about it, Jo. You didn't know what to think."

"I was hesitant, of course. But since I knew Gaby, your buddy, I got behind the idea…"

"The next morning, you bring me back by boat to Pointe-Rouge, where I jump in a tram and go downtown. From there, I make my way to the Saint-Charles Station, always walking on the sidewalk opposite the flow of traffic, so as not to get caught from behind. I get to the bottom of the great stairway on a side street. Three Krauts are pacing near the entrance, machine guns in hand. Impossible to change directions without looking suspicious. But people who walk with confidence are rarely stopped. *Grav*, you'd shown me the trick many times; now it was my turn to try… I make it! I quickly climb the stairs without even noticing how steep they are. The last flight: the station's rooftop appears just behind, then the entrance. Closely guarded, of course. I take a breather. I have to use the same tactic, there's no other choice. It works again, *Grav*! There, I'm inside. And then, damn! I get caught – only six days after my first arrest. I have time to throw my revolver in a garbage can. But I'm a real idiot: I still have my notebook and drafts in my coat pocket. Too late! When I see Gaby again (and it'll be the last time), I'll be wearing the same bracelet as him… You know the rest: destination Gestapo, Rue Paradis, where I see a good many of you: Paul, Raymond, *Grav*, Bonnet, Sandre, and poor Christian. That guy was there too, that sheep… What was his name again?"

"Moretti. At least, that's what he said."

Eugène remembered him clearly and told them the story of what happened upstairs, in my parents' empty apartment.

"Do we know what happened to him?"

"No idea."

Jo, who was never arrested and never sent to the STO due to his infirmity, will juggle grenades a while longer. Though he had to be more careful after the Corniche *blockhaus* incident, he still found a way to contact the fighters from "Combat," the biggest resistance organization in the unoccupied zone. A municipal employee like my father, he started making fake identification papers again, and made good use of the arms cache in the Saint-Pierre cemetery. Combat would distribute these precious weapons to the resistance cells of the Southeast FFI. These two tasks accomplished, Jo decided to spend his leisure time fishing. Without grenades – or almost. But he quickly got bored of this idle existence and soon joined a resistance cell in the Var.

As for Little Pierre, in good hands now, he let others decide his fate. "After Rue Paradis, it was the Fresnes prison, where I meet up with most of you. Then the Compiègne camp and finally Germany… Yes, we certainly took the five-star tour of Adolf's installations!"

❧ TWENTY-SIX ❧

My father's lost look. That way he had of suddenly leaving us to look beyond the present and fix his eyes, as if on a mirage, on a scene well behind him, in the haze of his past. One day, in the early eighties, we were in front of the Prefecture, on the terrace of a small bar where, as a young retiree, he'd often have a drink before his bus' departure, the "12:25." Flags flew from the top of the building in front of us, snapping in the wind, wrapping themselves around their mast, going from blue to white, and from white to red.

He suddenly emerged from his silence. "The shock, that morning in November 1942, when I arrived at the town hall for the day's work! There above the balcony, dancing in front of my eyes, an enormous flag, red like my shame…with a large white circle right in the middle…and in that circle, black like my anger, the arrogant spider that is the swastika. The bastards! That's where he'd brought France, the Old Puppet… Yet he'd still have the kids sing in school, 'Fly, dear flag / fly up high / France's icon / purveyor of hope.' You sang that in Moustiers, didn't you?"

"No, I don't think so. The teacher, Madame Dupuis, would make us sing *Maréchal, nous voilà*. Always following it with verse from *La Marseillaise*, though."

"A real disgrace for the country! Can you believe it? A government of rats elected by a majority of Frenchmen?"

Then he told me the story of the first visit Pétain made to Marseille as the newly named head of state, on the 3rd and 4th of December 1940.

"He was seen as a saviour by a defeated and discouraged population that swallowed all his nonsense whole. 'A partial occupation is better than a total occupation, we will be able to soften the conditions of the truce, our prisoners will return home soon...' The shield strategy, they called it! What baloney! 'A moral abuse of trust,' Blum said. Much easier to swallow words softened by patriotic spit than the words of an inflexible de Gaulle, determined to fight it out with Hitler's soldiers: 'France is not alone... This war is a world war... The flame of French resistance must not wane, nor shall it wane.'"

Very few were able to hear the June 18th declaration and even fewer actually listened to it. "By speaking to what is most desired by a man – the taste for rest – one always makes it easier on oneself. The desire for honour, though, does not come without a terrible price towards oneself and towards others."[9]

"And then there was Mers el-Kébir."

"Indeed, son. A disastrous English operation that de Gaulle had supported... A necessary evil. Nazi propaganda didn't miss the chance to blow it out of proportion and present it as a crime against France."

"Where were you on the 3rd of December?"

"At home. I was sleeping. I'd spent the night in town with *Le Grava*, Jo, Little Pierre, and a few others – sticking up pamphlets that we'd hastily prepared… *So that France may be victorious, England must!* With the cross of Lorraine on it… A few hundred of them…"

My dear Popaul's eyes would light up then: forty years younger all of a sudden.

"Where did you stick them?"

"Below the Canebière, on the Quai des Belges, and around here too, all around the Prefecture. We were sure that the official procession – the Marshal would be coming through the city in the days ahead – would go through one of those locations."

"Was it dangerous?"

"Not really. But there had been arrests in the preceding days – a few thousand undesirables, especially communists, who had been put inside for the duration of the celebrations – and the cops were on edge. We spent the night playing cat and mouse. And since it was my first mission, and I had a child at home, I was nervous."

"What was the result of your operation?"

"Good question. After the celebrations, most of the pamphlets were still where we put them. So they'd been read. Now, to maintain that our counter-propaganda had been effective… It would have taken much more than that to change public opinion. But it wasn't useless. Especially for us: it gave us the desire to continue and do more. We were ready for the Resistance."

In 1940, the French accepted, with a strong majority, to support the new State, falling into the trap of the lesser evil, refusing to see that it was essentially accepting the Nazi victory and, soon, their dictatorship. But a few of them who had their eyes open didn't see it in that way. I'm still proud today that my father was one of the righteous ones who chose the right camp: *Liberty, beloved Liberty!*

One day Doctor C. told me how my father had been recruited.

"He knew Jo, and Jo knew François. François, who had been my patient, was one of the first to join the cell, towards the end of 1940. He knew that both Jo and your father had reacted positively to the June 18th declaration and that they were hankering for some action… Maybe make their way to London to join the ranks of the Free French Forces. So it was François who brought them to me in January 1941. We were barely a half-dozen back then. In December, during the Marshal's visit to Marseille, they pasted up Gaullist pamphlets on the official route. During those sad days of hysteria, I was in the Saint-Pierre prison with other communist sympathizers. There were more than twenty thousand of us who'd been arrested to prevent any agitation."

"Twenty thousand!"

"Even more than that. In the Saint-Pierre prison and in the Chave prison too, in the city police stations and movies theatres. Even in boats. During that short stay in prison, I met Alfred, then a young officer. He was guarding us. We talked a little and I quickly understood where his sentiments lay. That's why, later that year, I went looking for him. Resistance movements were being born and I had decided to set up my own cell. I already had three men with me, Berthier and Armand, whom I met in Saint-Pierre, and my son Christian."

He motioned gently towards his son's portrait, as if the boy were really there.

"I recruited the first members of my network in prison, which just goes to show you that sometimes, good things come from adversity."

Then he took out a large format magazine, *L'Illustration,* dated December 14, 1940. Occupying the entire front page was a picture of the old Marshal, walking proudly at the head of the official procession. Beneath, the caption read, "Exiting the train station, Marshal Pétain reviews the honour guard."

"The caption is wrong. As you can see, they're in front of the Prefecture."

"Right, I recognize the place. How did the journalists make such a mistake?"

"Back then, authenticity was the least of their worries."

Four large pages, nine pictures, four of which showed a huge crowd. Plucking the petals of propagandist rhetoric, commenting with a touch of humour on its cheap lyricism, the doctor pointed out the tendentious aspect of a text that certainly fit the times.

Important news suddenly galvanized the sleeping city: Marshal Pétain, head of state, is arriving. Immediately, Marseille awakens, becomes animated, is reborn. For the past two days, all Provence has been making its way to the ancient Phocée. Hotels are refusing customers, streets are filled, building fronts are adorned. First, posters, flags, banners, festoons, garlands. [...] A blue sky woven from unreal silk, a powerful wind, almost warm, following a cold day. It seems as if even the sun of Provence wishes to celebrate the Marshal.

The doctor and the thousands of other potential opponents to the regime who'd been pushed aside, the closing of all cafés downtown, the colossal deployment of police forces, the exceptional security measures, the small pamphlets that contested the whole affair were not – of course – mentioned by the journalist. For him, everything was swell.

A huge crowd takes up position, in tight ranks, all along the Canebière and lines the vast open space – the Quai des Belges – that precedes the iridescent waters of the Old Port. Sun and smiles. Flags at every window, ribbons on every corsage – and people, countless people,

as have never been seen in Marseille, up to the cornice,
to the terraces, to the rooftops.

There, all is beauty and jubilation, calm and dignity when the first day in Marseille ends with "the deep and tumultuous voice of ships' sirens, the song of gold and blue waves that become iridescent with crimson in honour of the great red sun that sets and suddenly sinks behind the formidable black shadow of the Château d'If, crouching in the sea."

Nonsense! They tortured language to make it say what they wanted to hear.

After Marseille, Toulon. Same writer, same bombastic prose, perfectly adequate to the subject matter. On the battleship *Strasbourg*, where he reviews the crew, the Marshal stops for a second in front of the "right side of the hangar whose siding had been pierced by a falling shell on July 3, 1940, in Mers el-Kébir." For a moment, he "remains pensive in front of the injury sustained by the beautiful ship, then, with his clear look, he fixes his eyes on the stern where a flag that was torn by shards of metal, yet still floats in the breeze; it too was wounded in Mers el-Kébir."

After Toulon, Avignon. "The commander-in-chief of the French State continues his tour of France. Wherever he goes, he sows hope, faith, courage; he reanimates, he exalts, he encourages – in three words: he remakes France."

The doctor also dissected the pictures. "If the propaganda in the text is painfully obvious, that of the pictures is much more subtle. They are good documentary photos that display what is mentioned in their captions: the Marshal reviewing a company… a crowd gathered on the Quai des Belges… a visit to the Army of the Orient monument… But they also pass a strong emotional message. Without exaggerating too much, the photographer shows us the greatness of the Marshal and the high esteem in which a hoodwinked population holds him. Look at the one on the cover. Pétain stands at the tip of the triangle formed by the crowd watching the procession; he is shot from slightly underneath. He is saluting a row of militiamen fixed in perfect formation. His salute is energetic, elbow far from his body. He is advancing with firm steps, his eyes straight forward, determined, his mien is serious; the cane in his left hand is nothing but a prop. He doesn't lean on it. He looks good, the old chief! The flags we see in the background emerge over their heads, giving a positive feeling about the length of the procession. We have to make everyone forget about Montoire."

Montoire is a small city in the Loir-et-Cher *département*, near Vendôme. Pétain had met Hitler there six weeks prior, on October 24th. Their handshake, which shocked more than a few Frenchmen (the German press publicized it to the hilt), prefigured the Vichy regime's collaborationist policies. A fool's bargain would be struck: Germany held France at its mercy and the Marshal would become the Führer's puppet. In 1942, Pierre Laval would join in on the fun and start pulling the strings of the Old Puppet, playing the enemy's game with great talent.

"Look at how the point of view dominates the crowd. The framing is clever: the photo covers nearly the entire page; there are almost no margins. The effect is to makes us think of a human tide: people seem to be arriving from all sides at the same time."

A good photograph can be much more convincing than a bad article.

★

When I earned my *baccalauréat*, the doctor and his wife gave me a sumptuous present: *L'illustration* from December 14, 1940, and the *Pan Trilogy*, in a superb leather-bound edition, gold-lined… and signed by the author!

❧ TWENTY-SEVEN ❧

All that summer of 1945, my father and his friends would regularly meet up on Grandma Rose's terrace. As the moon slowly followed its path in the sky, towards the stars, they would remember their rare good moments – the soups they made, the cigarettes they shared – and especially their bad ones: the fevers, the typhus, the Homeric diarrheas. Each story would thumb its nose at death. I was terrified by some of them: the powerful jaws of the German shepherds, the Krauts' *gummi*, that truncheon lined with electrical cable covered in rubber. But I wouldn't have missed a single one of their heroic nights of recollection for all the chocolate in the world.

My fear would soon be conquered by the good humour of these fellows who, at every second word, would slap each other on the back. Today, it seems to me, all that energy was spent in the desire to forget: not to be thrown out of bed in the middle of the night by a voice barking orders, to achieve amnesia and close the Book of Horrors once and for all. They were trying to rebuild themselves and attain that wisdom that

Caraco preached. When you've seen with your own eyes a truck's exhaust feeding deadly gas into a shower room, when you've heard with your own ears the muffled cries emanating from a crematory oven and smelled with your own nose the smoke from the tall stacks with its sickening, sweet odour of silt that is the smell of burning flesh, what is there to fear? You might as well catch a cold.

Between them and myself, there was a closeness helped along by my father, a complicity that brought me much nearer to him, so much so that I sometimes forgot Moustiers and its charming little world for days on end.

When one of them would see Rose coming with a hot drink and a few bites to eat – "*Mèfi*, boys!" – the signal was given. All of them, recovering their old conditioned reflexes, would change the entire scene in a flash. Suddenly they became Zen, with smiles like the Buddha. They'd simulate reverie, hands behind their heads or folded on their stomachs, discussing some soothing subject. I quickly learned how to join in their nirvana, blissfully embedded in my chair.

When Henriette would come, the alert was quicker still. She was so sensitive, they'd have scared her stiff with their stories from another world.

And once the danger had passed, the question would be asked. "Now where were we?"

"You were talking about the role calls in the freezing cold... the Kommandos... the lice trade..."

"The lice trade? What's that, *Papa*?"

"You know the SS feared lice like the devil since they carried typhus and could contaminate them. Everywhere were signs saying, 'Eine Laus, deine Tod: a louse is your death!' That's why a single louse was worth a fortune: a whole day of *campo*!"

"*Campo*?"

"A day of rest, for disinfection."

And then the subject turned to the Sunday soup, as clear as every other day's, but in which a few pieces of meat floated – stringy meat that could only be dog. "At least it was nourishing!"

★

Horror stories made from witches' brew.

That shameless son who steals his father's bread, wolfs it down, then swallows his soup in a single gulp. To an indignant Caraco, the boy answers indifferently that his father is dying, so he no longer needs anything. The father looks on with resignation – not with supplication – he is beyond everything. Our very own preacher of non-violence punches the impious son, his just desserts. "*Brotdieb*! – Bread thief!" The most potent insult of all in a place where bread, as bad as it may be, was more than just coin, it was a symbol of life.

The well-trained dog, excited by its master, that in one terrifying bite rips out the throat of a "Muslim" lying on the ground. In the camps, the human rags that were no longer anything but skin over skeleton were called *Muselmänner*. With grace and dark humour, the prisoners granted Islamic fatalism – *inch Allah!* – to those who, devoured by the demons of hunger, wandered in a daze, looking for something to eat – anything, really: roots, grass, leaves, paper, rotting wood…

In the Buchenwald quarry. A prisoner, carrying a stone weighing several kilos on his shoulder, collapses, exhausted. An SS officer approaches, takes his *luger* out and presses it against the forehead of the poor man, who tenses his eyelids till tears flow and he wets his pants… The SS officer changes his mind and holsters his gun. The condemned man opens his eyes, smiling to the heavens. But the SS calls a Kapo over to finish the job for him. The Kapo comes running, bends over the man, throwing his *gummi* aside, and takes him by the neck with both hands. Throttles him with all his might. An empty body now. The master appreciates the show, the student is proud; they understand each other.

And then, of course, the punishment of the post, which of the boys, only Alexandre had suffered. It was in Dachau. He was tied, hands behind his back, to a chain tied to a hook, then forced to climb a stepladder that was pulled out from under him. A violent shock for the shoulders. "You swung a few centimetres from the ground, trying to lean forward as much as possible, to avoid having your arms go too far back." But little by little, resistance would wane, and the hanged man would end up in complete extension, incredibly painful. He'd faint and have a pail of freezing water thrown on him. Duration of the punishment: one hour. After that, it lost its efficiency. From fainting to the pail of water, the poor man would usually enter a catatonic state that would inhibit all pain. Or sometimes he'd simply be dead.

Some of the other boys had experienced the punishment of the stool, a softer version of the post. My father was a regular customer. "For the slightest thing, they'd make you climb onto a high narrow stool. You had to stay there, squatting on the tip of your toes, arms pointing out at shoulder level... For a quarter of an hour! Mission impossible: muscle fatigue would quickly make you tumble off your perch. Two or three tumbles, and the acrobatics would always end with a most substantial reward – twenty-five blows from the *gummi* across your back. Offered with much generosity."

The Dachau infirmary, the *Revier*. Fred wandered in with a nail infection on the middle finger of his left hand. He was in tremendous pain and couldn't work. He left the infirmary a few days later, able to work – with a finger less. "Heiden operated on me. No anaesthesia, of course; they had to save their ethyl chloride. Just a punch in the chin to knock me out when I started screaming too loudly." Josef Heiden? A Kapo who had the *Revier* SS's permission to do whatever he wanted and who terrorized both patients and nurses by trying out surgery from time to time. Fred was furious. "A monster of perversion who beat the SS at their own game, a vampire thirsting for blood, Heiden was!" Impossible to describe him without abusing clichés and hyperbole, though words would never come close to the odious reality of the man. "It wouldn't have been better if I'd had a real surgeon. Either they sent novices who needed experience before going to the front lines or experienced doctors doing research for the Nazi war medicine."

Never think of those horrors again…

One last story has never left me; it has a hold on me like the jaws of a German shepherd. In the rare cases when a miracle-man managed to survive the treatment inflicted, Josef Heiden would be called in again to quickly clean up the mess. He'd finish his executioner's job by rolling his victims in a blanket, then placing them under a freezing shower for some time. Then, tightly bound in their blankets that would shrink as they dried, the poor men were dumped in a corner of a room where, shaking uncontrollably, they would die, tetanized, in horrible convulsions.

★

One mid-August night, I remember it well. The moon was high and full like a large white stain over the Frioul Islands. That night, the laughter had quickly been overshadowed by an embarrassed, heavy conversation.

"We know who!" my father declared. We: he and Little Pierre. What did they know? An enormous secret that had been at the centre of many discussions in the Blocks of the various camps where they lived out their fragile existence. They knew who had given them up – my father never said "ratted them out." He and Pierre knew who'd sent twenty-one of them to their deaths.

"What? You know the son of a bitch and you haven't said anything?"

"Wait, Sandre. Imagine if it was one of us..."

My father's words froze me to the marrow. Around me were dumbstruck faces.

"And imagine," Little Pierre went on, "that the man broke under torture on Rue Paradis..."

He could evoke torture with poignant intensity. "Barbary in its purest form! Imagine, facing you, a sinister face that intends one thing and that's to reduce you to a pulp. A face as tight as a fist that will relax only at the sound of your cries. You try to resist as much as possible, you want to hide any sign of distress that would only serve to heighten your torturer's cruelty. A one-sided heroic battle where every blow is directed at you. Finally, the moment comes when you lose all strength and faint – a real luxury! But the pails of freezing water thrown in your face quickly return you to the harsh reality of your position. Hang on a minute more, do not give in... but for how long?"

"But wait a minute... If it was on Rue Paradis, before our arrests, then it's got to be..."

My father interrupted Alexandre. His deductions were leaping too far ahead of the conversation.

"You have to remember, Sandre, how it was on Rue Paradis. There was Tortora with his heavy hands. And Max the

Pervert… You must remember him, right? He had a particular affection for you…"

Alexandre did remember. I could read it on his face. Paler than the descending moon…you could measure the cruelty of the humiliation inflicted on a man as proud as he was – a "native of Calenzana," as he liked to introduce himself. He wasn't the only one who still carried, somewhere on his body, the scars of cigarette burns, for Max the SS enjoyed stubbing out his smoke on some particularly sensitive part of the body. My Popaul had his around his nipples: three or four stigmata on each side – well-aimed shots.

"So," he continued, "if you'd broken down, Sandre? Or you, Raymond?"

"I'd have killed myself!"

"That's what he did. But slowly, staying with us until the end and letting his remorse eat him up slowly. It took two years…"

"Two years watching you waste away next to him; he resigned himself to his suffering as a form of expiation," Caraco added. He probably had no idea who the man might be, since he came from a cell in the Var region.

"He died in our arms, in Dachau," Little Pierre remembered, "two weeks before liberation."

"He gave us his secret at the last moment. Then he left us, relieved, his eyes burning with tears of gratitude when we promised never to say anything to his wife."

"Madeleine?"

"Yes, Madeleine."

"So it was Armand! You did well, boys. May he rest in peace."

Caraco had just understood, too. A forgiving silence settled over the group for the rest of the night.

One month later, Madeleine received the Legion of Honour in the name of her glorious late husband. Posthumously. The doctor, who had to leave his son's body in Dachau, managed to find the strength to say a few moving words to her. The boys congratulated her and embraced her affectionately.

★

The regulars met on the terrace all the way into mid-September, until the night Caraco arrived alone, without Raymond.

They both lived near the Old Port and took the tramway together to the square Joseph-Étienne, then climbed the Rue des Lices slope and the long Rue Chaix staircase. Raymond always arrived out of breath due to his pneumothorax. But that didn't stop him from picking me up by the armpits as soon as he arrived, holding me at arm's length and asking, "How are you, kid?" Since he was the only one who couldn't kiss me, that was his way of showing affection. His red face radiated kindness, his deep-set eyes kept a youthful glint, and the smile that displayed his overly long teeth should have scared me, but instead it would turn up the sides of his lips and give him a humorous look. Even though at that time I was as "long as a day without bread" (Grandma Rose always used that expression), the effort that Raymond made picking up my twenty kilos exacerbated the whistle of his locomotive breathing. My father would always tell him, "Don't do that, Momon! Your doctor told you not to expend unnecessary energy." He'd answer with a shrug of his shoulders and a broad smile. Once – and it's remained etched in my memory – he answered while gasping for breath, "Unnecessary? What's unnecessary? This is Life, Paul... that I'm holding in my arms." Those weak arms worried me the most; I was afraid they would break under my weight.

But that day, Caraco was alone.

"What about Raymond?"

"He isn't well. Tomorrow he goes back to the clinic. They're going to try a new medication that's supposed to be really effective. It's called streptomycin..."

"He's going back to hospital?"

"Yes."

"Won't he come back to see us?"

"Yes, later, when he's better."

My father's answer did nothing to reassure me. I could hear the lack of conviction in his voice.

That night was like any other night under the stars. Besides my father and Caraco, Little Pierre was there, always the first to arrive since he lived next door on Rue du Coteau. François

Le Grava was there, with Jo the *Goï* and Fred. That night, they mostly spoke of Raymond.

Le Grava told how they'd almost gotten into a fight when the doctor had assigned this greenhorn to a mission with our Robin Hood – the type he preferred to execute alone. He'd spoken some hurtful words to the inexperienced young whippersnapper who still had peach fuzz on his cheeks. Raymond was barely eighteen in 1943 – twelve years younger than *Le Grava*. It made no sense to go in broad daylight with a beginner to a rail yard full of boxcars – and soldiers – to take stickers off train cars that read "Sisteron lamb for Munich" and "Brignoles bauxite for Düsseldorf" or into the middle of the city to blow up electrical pylons and transformers. But the doctor knew what he was doing. And in the end, *Le Grava* couldn't speak highly enough of the kid full of courage and determination. It was the beginning of a solid, sincere but much too short friendship.

Then my father told of that horrible scene in Dachau. The camp had just been liberated by American troops, and ghosts were rummaging through every part of it, searching for food and "interesting" objects abandoned by the Nazis. My father laughed at his own foolishness. Like many others, he filled a large bag: cameras, pistols, daggers, badges… But the bag was too heavy for his frail body, stricken by typhus, and his treasure proved too heavy to carry. No sooner had he finished gathering up his loot than he had to abandon it.

A few minutes later, exhausted, he was leaning against a wall with Raymond near their Block. Sitting a couple metres away, a Russian prisoner was attempting to open a can with a screwdriver. The contents of the can had moved when he'd shaken it, and he thought there might be soup or fruit juice inside. Raymond was able to read the label: *Tischlerleim*. "Damn! It's glue!" He ran to the starving man and tried to explain his mistake to him. But the Russian misinterpreted his intentions, figuring Raymond wanted to take his treasure away. Raymond insisted, doing all he could to explain the situation, just as the other man managed to open the lid.

It came to fists. A bit of glue ran down Raymond's arm; it had a good almond smell. The Russian was much stronger than his presumed aggressor. He put down the can but still held the screwdriver. Not too fast on his feet, Raymond came near to meeting his end. Like a St. Bernard mixed with a pit bull, he refused to give up his dangerous mission, and my father had a hard time separating him from the man who had no intention of being robbed.

The Russian calmed down and returned to his spot, where he wolfed down what he thought was a godsend with small moans of pleasure. Resigned, the two friends could only watch him sink into fatal gluttony.

His guts couldn't take the meal. He died half an hour later in horrible intestinal pain. Raymond held him in his arms, his eyes full of compassion, and accompanied him to the distant border of his ancestral Siberia. "That's how Momon is: determined, courageous, generous…" my father spoke.

He would use those same epithets a week later, on September 22nd, but in a sentence spoken in the past tense. It was in front of Raymond's tombstone. I too wanted to accompany him with the others to his final resting place. Along the walkways of the cemetery where my grandmother held my hand, each of us followed the ceremony with heads bent to hide our tears.

Raymond's shade threw a shroud over the heavens. The boys lost their taste for jokes. The season of starry nights on Rose and Henriette's terrace would end long before the first cold days of autumn.

❧ TWENTY-EIGHT ❧

Much later, in our private moments, my father took to being rather sparing in his confidences, and I was reluctant to question him about his past suffering. Yet one day, when his doctor had just advised him to have an operation on his injured leg – rebreaking the tibia, realigning it, then a simple ablation of the meniscus, nothing out of the ordinary – he admitted that, in the camps, that injury had been ceaseless torture. "It was painful, believe me. Especially mornings, when I had to get up. Then once we started walking, there was no way to slow down and rest. Not being able to keep up meant the death penalty, for inability to work." A bullet in the back of the neck; the stragglers were left on the side of the road. "More than once the boys held me up… they put me back on my own two feet." Then he winked. As a typical man of Marseille, he loved word play, even the weak kind – especially when it thumbed its nose at death. "At night, the same show, different time… When I could finally lie down and try to forget the day's horrors, I wouldn't find peace for long. Rare were the nights when my leg didn't poison my sleep. Once I was asleep, the blows, the fatigue, it would all return and make me suffer again, nightmares more real than life. Not to mention the parasites and the numerous skin ailments – scabies, erysipelas, impetigo, prurigo, eczema…"

Then my father would fall silent. I remembered the images from back on the Marseille terrace. Did he have a bed? You couldn't call it that. A blanket that was never changed, never washed, a meagre mattress filled with wood chips that had turned to dust eons ago. Regular parasite nests – lice, bedbugs, acaroids of every kind. Even some rather bizarre ones like the "Adolf bug," so named for the swastika-shaped stripes in the centre of its chitinous armour. At lights out, all those crawlers would be ready to go, sharpening formidable weapons – darts, stingers, mandibles, hooks. They would begin their conquest of the hosts they found to be the tenderest of meats and in whose folds of skin they would find cover until the first light of day.

Then, joking, my father would add, "You know, in the end, the German that stole my basil and my Parmesan when we were arrested couldn't have imagined the favour he was doing me. Though I went hungry, those two simple ingredients continued to exist in my mind, and my imagination multiplied them. Like Christ and the loaves and fishes. They made dozens of delicious *pistous*, smooth and flavourful. I offered them to whoever asked. Even Eugène wouldn't have refused."

In their starved hallucinations, each of them had their favourite meal. I can remember Little Pierre's performance, one night on the terrace. He told us that his trick was to mime the devouring of a steak cooked to perfection. This demonstration followed: with his thumb and index finger well parted, his left hand hefted the lovely thickness of the slab of meat. Then, with the skill of a matador, his right hand impaled it with a fork – "made of finest Toledo steel," he added, thrusting out his chest with all the dignity of a Spanish hidalgo. He followed up with his knife, which sliced through the meat like butter. "The meat is tender," he declared, in case we hadn't understood, then cut off a huge piece. His fork delivered it to his gaping mouth and *snap*! It closed. His jaw went into action then: a meticulous mastication that deformed the flexible contour of his face. His temples beat like a heart – diastole, systole. His gullet went up and down with a gourmand's deglutition, eyes half-closed. After patting the corners of his mouth with his napkin, he recovered his usual face. Then, of course, the exaggerated sigh: "Aaaaah…" End of scene. Eugène laughed heartily in appreciation. Encore!

Masochism is often a source of pleasure.

★

My dad's been gone for more than twenty years. Of all the boys he fought alongside, the only one to have made it to the new millennium is Little Pierre, today a young octogenarian.

He still lives in Marseille, and I always visit him when I'm there. Still loves the theatre just as much, and just like my father, he too balks at evoking the dark years.

After those nights during the summer of 1945, the boys still wanted to participate in the official commemorations, chests thrust out under the heavy collection of medals, mirroring the rays of the sun. They worked within their beloved FNDIR (the National Federation for Deportees and Internees of the Résistance) to preserve the memory of their comrades who had died for the country. Yet, privately, the time to discuss their own sacrifices was past. They'd had the terrace to speak the unspeakable to those who could understand. Now, there was forgetting.

Until the day when Pierre, nearly forty years later, shortly after my father's death…

"This is for you, Dominique. I found it at the Federation when I was working in the archives."

I immediately recognized the writing, spiked like an electrocardiogram. These were notes scribbled down on Hôtel Lutetia letterhead.

"It's my father! Can I keep them?"

"You may. I've made a photocopy. It's his itinerary. It's also Raymond's and mine. After Fresnes, we were never separated, the three of us."

"What about the doctor?"

"The doctor, Christian, and François – and Alexandre too – hooked up with us in Buchenwald, a few months later. That's where we met Caraco. In Dachau, our last stop, only eight of us from the original cell were left... We knew about Christian through his father. As for the others – Borel, Bonnet, Autran – we knew nothing."

Paris, June 7, 1945

On November 29, 1943, after a few months stay in the Fresnes prison, I was transferred to the Neue Bremm camp in Sarrebruck. Pierre and Raymond are in the same convoy. As we exit the train, there's about forty of us boys chained two by two and packed in a prison car, urged along by blows from the guards' cudgels. Arrive at the camp after a half-hour ride.

A small, dreadful place. Daily diet: 1 litre of foul-tasting herb soup and 100 grams of some viscous black bread. Daily entertainment: after the morning roll call that can last hours, we must jog around a basin, then crawl several metres in the mud, then walk while squatting with our hands behind our heads, under a shower of blows from a bullwhip My leg is horribly painful. The stragglers are clubbed to death.

We're transferred to Buchenwald in the heart of winter. Long ride in cattle cars. At arrival, sent to disinfection. Being dunked, head and all, in a bathtub filled with purple-blue water that has permanganate poured in. Dressed in rags afterwards: the striped pajama is reserved for transport and work outside the camp. Then sent to the Quarantine Block. We find the doctor, Christian, Sandre, and François there... together with an eccentric, Ludovic Caraco.

During quarantine, every day, after interminable roll calls (many die of the cold), we leave for the quarry, two kilometres away. We each take a rock weighing several kilograms that we bring back to the camp. Time and time again. At the end of day, we suffer through a grotesque inspection: paraded nude in front of an SS who turns us every which way with the tip of his rod, looking for lice. Then, time out in the Block, packed like animals, sleeping on bunks crawling with vermin.

We stay several months in Buchenwald. I work at the station with Raymond, unloading cars filled with glass wool and loading them with coal. Many comrades die of exposure.

In July 1944, transferred to Natzwiller-Struthof camp in Alsace, together with Pierre, Raymond, and Sandre. Confined to Block 14, which belongs to the NNs. Meet up with Armand and Berthier. Each day, we break rocks, dig ditches, transport large wheelbarrows full of earth over many metres: many die of exhaustion. Comrades from the Alliance cell who were in the Schirmeck camp a few kilometres from ours are brought to Struthof and hung on hooks in a room adjacent to the crematory ovens. We wait our turn. Not yet: faced with the advancing Allied army, the camp is quickly evacuated. Saved in extremis from a horrible death.

In September, we are evacuated once again, this time to Dachau. Packed in cattle cars, 120, 140 men in each. Many suffocate.

Soon enough, we are sent in a Kommando to Freiburg. Leave at six in the morning, come back at six at night. Several kilometres to reach our workplace. My leg, always…

A few weeks later, typhus appears in the camp. We are sent in February 1945 to Vaihingen, near Stuttgart.

In March, evacuation again: de Lattre is at Stuttgart's doors. Back to Dachau. Always the godforsaken cattle cars: two-day trip, many don't make it. Christian dies.

In the camp, we are saved due to a providential coal shortage. Armand dies in our arms.

April 29th. Finally liberated by the Americans! Those who have typhus (Pierre, Raymond, Sandre, and I) are quarantined in the camp's SS barracks. Still, many die, despite our liberators' care.

June 2nd. Repatriated to Paris and sent to the Hôtel Lutetia. Maguy, Ange and Georges still alive, eleven of us at the Lutetia!

❧ TWENTY-NINE ❧

When I took Nela to Moustiers for the first time, five years ago, I hadn't set foot there myself in more than twenty-five years. Not since I'd moved to Toronto. We wanted to visit Antoine first. The Audibert family has been making faience from one generation to the next for just about forever, and the Riou Workshop where Gérard and I used to have *carte blanche* was one of the most fascinating places of our childhood.

These days, with expressways that run almost half the distance, the village is only about an hour's ride from Marseille. We left right after lunch and arrived near the village in early afternoon.

Past Riez, right after a turn, Moustiers-Sainte-Marie appears suddenly, nestled between the rocks, with its tile roofs in tight rows like an army ready to conquer the mountain along the break in its rock face.

"A real postcard! It reminds me a little of the village of Monchique in the Algarve. We've never been there together. When I was a little girl, we spent our summers there with my cousins."

I had the same feeling. A distant signal warned me I was entering the land of my childhood.

Better than a postcard: an authentic masterpiece, in contrasts, painted with a palette knife, with thick slabs of colour. A canvas on which all the details have been chosen and orchestrated to celebrate the great festival of colours and lines with a maximum of plasticity and radiant intensity.

Ah, the colours. The yellow and ochre of the rocks breaking into the bright blue of the sky. The green smudges of vegetation – from the deepest green, a bouquet of cypress and yew surrounding a small chapel perched over the village, to the brilliant green of the prairie in the foreground; but also the silver-tinged green of the olive trees that stipple the surrounding slopes. Then comes the steel grey of a line of willow and poplar trees that cross sideways through the lower part of the painting.

The lines, then. A few curves, mostly verticals rushing toward the sky like prayers. A broken line at the very top triumphs: the rocky crest, collapsed in the middle, its peak seemingly cut with a billhook.

Sometimes a landscape can speak for the state of your soul.

"Let's stop a moment."

I stopped the car on the side of the road, right next to a young fig tree that gladly offered us its sweet-smelling fruit (Nela loves figs). Less subtle were its neighbours, a shrub of broom and a tuft of lavender that sent their intoxicating perfumes pouring over us.

At that very moment, having come close enough during the drive, in the centre of the landscape, we saw the star suspended on its chain, pulling together the two sides of the mountain.

We started down on the road again. A first kilometre, lined with willow and poplar. Another, with chestnut trees. Then another still, shaded by almond trees and subtly scented lindens.

We negotiated the last hairpin curve – look, the still is gone, but the tall walnut tree hasn't moved – and the last straight line that brought us to the village square where it was easy to park since the tourists hadn't shown up yet. No one on the square: the village was heavy with sleep. Alone on the bridge that leads to the square stood an old man, hands in his pockets, eyes lost in the distance. We stopped a few metres away so as not to trouble his meditation and leaned on the balustrade to silently contemplate the stream tumbling down the deep ravine.

We went in search of a hotel and chose the Belvédère, less for its attractive menu with the Michelin star that was posted by the door than for its position on the edge of the rocky spur.

"Room number 3." From our room, the view was extraordinary, broader still than the one from the bridge. The same view that, ages ago, we had from the small upstairs room. We gazed at the impressive panorama, decorated with lush purple waves – it would be another two months before the lavender would be ready for harvesting – all the way to the bluish hills of the horizon. These days, there were no fighter planes in the sky.

"Do you like it?"

"It's very nice. The bed seems comfy, and the view… By the way, that star must have quite a story…"

"*Té, pardi!* Quite a story indeed, and historic, too!"

As he put on a large white apron, our host at the hotel – he was also the cook and owner of the Belvédère – launched into a story, apocryphal, no doubt, of the local lord who left for the first Crusades, first promising a lady of Moustiers that upon his return from the holy war, he would bring back a star and, to honour her, would hang it, yes indeed, on a heavy chain between the two sides of the mountain. And the lady apparently encouraged him with these words: "Return as a victor, valiant knight, and you shall have my heart. But return defeated…" – our storyteller paused here for effect – "and you shall have nothing. Do not imagine you may return empty-handed for, consider it, how could you then honour your promise?"

I spoke to the innkeeper of my youth. We were about the same age but didn't know each other. He'd come to Moustiers a dozen years before. He was originally from L'Isle-sur-la-Sorgue, in the Vaucluse – "the homeland of the poet René Char," he added with ostensible pride, then recited in grand style:

Camped on the hillsides above the village are fields of mimosa. During the season of harvest, it may happen that

you meet an extremely sweet-smelling girl whose arms have
been busy all day among the fragile branches. Like a lamp
with a bright nimbus of perfume, she goes on her way, her
back to the setting sun.

To speak to her would be sacrilege.

Her slippers tread upon the grass. Let her pass. You may
be lucky enough to sense the chimaeras of the dew on her lips.
Wind Away.[10]

What is the link between this poem and Moustiers? None at all. Simply pride in its purest form: to come from a landscape that produced such a poet!

"I'm sure you know my friend Antoine Audibert."

"*Boudiou*, Toinou! He's my *pétanque* partner. As good a shooter as a maker of faience – the best in Moustiers and the whole region! His workshop is just five minutes away, above the village. Cross the bridge and the Couvert Square, turn right, go up Rue de la Diane past the church, and you'll be at the Montée de la Clappe that leads to the Riou falls. Well, it's right there, on your right, the Riou Workshop. You'll see it easy enough."

"Thanks, I know the place. We'll go right away."

"Right away? *Capoun*, you haven't been back here in a blue moon…"

"Yes, and…?"

"You're forgetting the *sieste* – it's naptime, *pardiéu!* The *sieste* is sacred around here… You won't find Antoine anywhere before four o'clock. He chose the right profession, he did. As you can see, no *sieste* for me. I'm just about to head to the kitchen. If you want to have supper here tonight – I'm making wild boar stew! It's been marinating since yesterday morning. We serve supper from seven-thirty to nine-thirty only. It's still off-season for at least another week."

"We don't know what we'll do tonight. For Antoine, not before four, is that it?"

"Four or four-thirty."

"Well, if Antoine is having his *sieste*, we'll do the same."

"Right you are. An hour of sleep never hurt, eh?"

We lingered a moment, leaning by the open window, looking at the multicoloured checkerboard of the landscape, counting fields of lavender and grain, tracing the flow of streams with our fingers – the Riou (trout) that flows into the Adou and the Adou (crawfish) into the Maïre, its own waters reaching the Verdon. These scenes are such a part of me that when I describe them to Nela, I'm describing myself.

Four-thirty. We left the hotel under a bright sun, the undisputed master of the skies. The church bell sounded once, echoing against the flank of the mountains; it came back to us as a vibrato. We crossed the bridge once again and made our way through the square, which had now become a meeting place for the entire village. The conversations sometimes had a bit of Provençal in them, and they were always punctuated with expansive hand gestures.

"Do you hear the *ing* of the local dialect? The sound rises into the air like balloons, while their *eu* and their *ang*, much heavier, tumble like the river down a ravine."

Oh, Holy Mother of Marseille, the ache of having a linguist for a wife! Nela took her revenge for the *eich* and the *aouch* I point out in the *palabras* I hear when we visit her native Portugal.

On the other side of the Place du Couvert lies Hamel's butcher shop. The opulence on display there paradoxically reminds me of the time when, in the middle of an almost empty window, we could read a message on a slate that informed the customers of the endemic shortages. During the war, a time when France was systematically exploited by Nazi Germany, goods were conspicuous by their absence. But today... With parsley filling its nostrils, posing on a wide white plate is a pig's head that seems to be smiling at a decapitated sheep that lost its skin at the slaughterhouse, its thorax open, hanging pitifully from a hook. Next to it, also hung vertically and carved up, two bug-eyed rabbits nose-dive towards the grinning pig. A capon hanging from its legs shows off its sprinter's thighs; a garland of sausages hangs around it, beckoning to me: "Eat us! Eat us!" "No way! Speak to me of *chouriço*, and you might have an audience. Those aren't even smoked!" Nela's taste clearly points towards the large piece of raw ham on the left that she stubbornly calls *presunto*.

The Rue de la Diane, then the church. On its stairs, a panhandler clearly unconcerned about his begging bowl sleeps in the shade, stretched out like a cat, his hands over his chest in the august position that characterizes recumbents. Sacred *sieste*!

"Dominique, I can't decipher the plaque over the fountain."

"It says it's the starting point of the *diane*."

"The *diane*?"

"Back in the day, in the army, the *diane* was the bugle blow that sounded at dawn to wake the soldiers. It was called 'sounding the *diane*.'"

"Nobody says that anymore?"

"No. But it was still used in my grandfather's time. Today, we just call it the reveille. Here in Moustiers, the word now refers to a small troop of five or six musicians – fifes, pipes, drums and folkloric dress. They leave from here, the church steps, on the day of the votive celebration, and they serenade the town. At five in the morning."

"Too early for me. What were the votive celebrations like when you were a child?"

"Religious and pagan, in that order. They would start the preceding evening with a procession. At ten-thirty, we'd meet near the church's lesser door, on the other side, which gives onto the square. The whole village would be carrying lanterns, torches, multicoloured paper lanterns…"

"*Lampiões*, made from pleated paper with a candle inside?"

"Exactly. And the whole troop, with the priest in front, would make its way to the Notre-Dame-de-Beauvoir chapel."

"You'd climb all the way up?"

"Indeed, while singing canticles, to boot. Three hundred and sixty-five steps, one for each day of the year, to reach the top – not much fun, I'll tell you that! But we would stop at every station, and there are twelve on the way up."

"And once you got there?"

"Once we made it, we kids would swing on the bell rope – *balalìn, balalan* – until the priest would tell us to stop, just before midnight, to say mass. Once it was over, the procession would reform and we'd go down the steps, in the dark, with our torches and lanterns lighting our way."

"You'd go to bed late!"

"Around two or three. A lot of people would stay up and wait for the *diane*. The next morning, though, we had to be on the church square at ten sharp for the *pétanque* game. It would end in mid-afternoon. A few hours of *sieste* and then, *rascle!* back to the church square where a platform had been set up the day before for a band – a real one – with four or five musicians. A handsome platform crowned with foliage – holly, mistletoe, ivy, rosemary… First came the singing contest at eight o'clock, then *balèti*, dancing, around ten. In their Sunday clothes, big and small would dance together, all of us: the baker with the hairdresser, the butcher-woman with the policeman, Émile with Marie, Mireille with Roger…"

"And you and Dany."

"Not always."

"What about school? You must have needed a few days of rest after such celebrations."

"School didn't start until October back then, and the celebrations were in September."

Another twenty metres and we came upon the *Clappe* trail.

"A *clappe*?"

"A *clappe* is, uhh…"

"You don't even know what it is!!"

"*Vé*! It's this, in front of us… Look, there's the Atelier du Riou! The door is open, let's go in."

In the middle of the shop, a friendly octogenarian with her white hair pulled into a bun was showing a pair of elderly tourists around, ahead of the hordes of summer tourists. They were hesitating over several large pieces.

"It's for our grandniece, you see, she's getting married next month."

"Take your time. It's a difficult choice, but you can't go wrong. All three pieces are wonderful."

Indeed, a fruit bowl, a vase, and a planter: "wonderful" is the word. The faience was nicely displayed on shelves throughout the store, some hanging on walls, the larger pieces set on a heavy oak table. In one corner, on an old dough trough (copiously rubbed with bee's wax, considering its sheen) were a group of practical objects – salad bowls, mortar and pestles for garlic mayonnaise, bottle openers – made from olive or vine wood. But what attracted Nela's attention, sitting since time immemorial on the same table near the entrance: the *toupin*!

"Look how beautiful that baking tray is! It's wonderful, don't you think?"

"Indeed! It's a Joseph Olerys *toupin*. Antoine's grandfather bought it at the beginning of the century."

"You knew him?"

"The grandfather? Yes, I knew him. He died in the sixties."

"Joseph Olerys, *parvo!*"

"I know a little of his story. He was born in Marseille in the late seventeenth century, and did his painter's apprenticeship (probably at the Clérissy's, faience-makers who were in vogue back then) before founding his own workshop in Alcora, under a Spanish lord. He then moved to Moustiers in 1738, where he introduced the polychromatics. He stayed here until his death in 1748. As for his *toupin*, it's always stood right here."

"A magnificent piece!"

Assuredly so. A "*grand feu*" faience, meaning that the paint was applied after a first baking. It is some thirty centimetres high, with two handles and a cover. And a decoration of blue, orange, and green garlands on a blue-tinged white background, as clear as a child's eyes. The handles show horrific heads – half-man, half-lion – of comical ugliness, wearing Pharaonic headbands with orange stripes. Mounted on the cover is a pine cone with orange scales. And, around the circumference, a mythological scene repeated four times: two mermaids with superbly pointed breasts sit haughtily enthroned on a rock, defying the waves breaking at their feet.

Not for sale, of course. "And do not touch us, please! We cost a lot and are not for sale."

The tourists, from Belgium, if I was to believe my ears, decided to take the planter. Expertly swaddled in fine paper, delicately placed in a cardboard box, buried under an avalanche of polystyrene bits. "*Té!* So you don't risk any damage on the way back."

They paid and left with a few kind words.

"Good afternoon. I see you like the dough trough there. Unfortunately it's not for sale. For the same reason as the *toupin* by the entrance. I saw it also interested you. They've been in the family for at least one hundred and fifty years. But this beautiful mortar and pestle – carved out of olive wood from a tree one hundred years old – they can be yours if you want them. With a tool like that, you'll never spoil a single garlic sauce, I'll guarantee that. Here, everything gets better with age. Look at me, eighty-five next month!"

"Bah, I'm sure that isn't true, more like twenty-five, if you ask me! What's your secret?"

"It's the air here, my dear, and the water. Everything is pure in Moustiers."

"The village water comes from a spring that flows right near here, next to the rocks in the valley. We'll go see it afterwards."

"See it and taste it, I hope! And this salad bowl, do you like it? Also made of olive wood. The olive tree is Provence's standard, as Giono said. It'll look great on a beautiful tablecloth made from local fabric."

She pointed to her apron, a streak of colour over a black dress. From the colour of her cloth to that of the faience around us, the visit was tinted with the glow of my childhood.

"On this side of the shop, you have your traditional Moustiers faience. This is a pretty motif of fantasy creatures in the Bérain style from the early eighteenth century, inspired by the *Commedia dell'Arte*. The other side is different, more modern. Mostly polychromatic motifs."

From casseroles to ewers, we'd soon looked at every piece of pottery in the store.

"These insect and wildflower motifs are really quite nice."

"They're original creations from our master faience-maker, Antoine Audibert."

"And he's the one we've come to see. You don't recognize me, Madame Audibert?"

"No…"

"Émile and Marie's nephew?"

"*Boudi*! You're Dominique, the nephew of poor Émile and poor Marie?"

"Yes, Mireille's son. And this is my wife Nela."

"A pleasure."

"The pleasure is mine, my dear lady. *Aquest'aco*! Come and let me kiss you, Dodo, *moun bèu*! Tell me, your mother, how is she?"

"So-so. She's sad."

"How old is she now?"

"Ninety next year."

"It's true, there are almost five years... We were really quite sad, you know, for Gérard. We saw him only a bit before. So thin, *pécaïré*! Death... *qué tarasque, qué putarasse*! So young... Only two years older than my Toinou... He's working next door, I'll go get him for you."

Our embrace had the warmth of good bread straight from the oven. We didn't want to break off that embrace. "*Fan de chine*, you haven't changed a bit, Dodo!" "And look at you, Toinou, you look the same!" It would be sad indeed if, between friends, you couldn't lie a little.

Under the spell of Olerys, Nela finally decided to buy a traditional soup tureen, one of Antoine's works. Quite beautiful, with a fantasy motif in blue monochrome – the same tureen we still have today, in Toronto.

★

If my reunion with Antoine and his mother was uplifting, my walk through the village, a bit later, was quite different.

On every corner, I expected to see him again. At the fountain, bent under the weight of the watering can he'd come to fill. On the church square, in the first row of the crowd surrounding the *pétanque* players. Everywhere his image, his presence, as surprising as a slap in the face when he'd want to wake me up: "Are you dumb or something,

Dodo?" Bent over the bridge railing, throwing pebbles into the rushing waters below. In school, holding Dany in his arms… Gérard the great, the generous, the impish – all at the same time.

"Your old school is completely new!"

"It was rebuilt in exactly the same place as the old one. One, two, three: three classrooms now."

"You stayed here until June of 1945?"

"Yes. After that I went to Marseille. In October, at the start of the new year, I went to Saint-Victor school with Gérard, just in front of the church, where there's a small square now."

"With that plaque honouring the Resistance fighter, the Companion of the Liberation?"

"Berthe Albrecht, killed in 1945."

"Your father knew her?"

"I don't think so. They didn't really know anyone outside of their cells."

"How long did you stay at that school?"

"Only a semester, until the end of 1945, when my father left Rue Chaix. In a few months, he put on several kilos and his health progressed quickly. It was a strange reunion with a new character from my life. He had deserted his own portrait, then ended up resembling it as he nursed himself back to health. One day, he came out of his room dressed as a sailor: it was a total success… In January of 1946, he was offered a post at Veterans Affairs."

"What kind of post?"

"For six months, he was the director of a reception centre for returning deportees who hadn't yet found their families. A large building – previously a spa – in Camoins, a small village not far from Marseille."

"And what did you do?"

"I returned to live with my mother, who'd settled down in Aubagne with Roger."

"Now, Dominique, why don't you take me to the Riou waterfalls?"

First down Caterwaul Lane.

Gérard was still there, shirt open, hair blowing in the wind, a single lock over the left eye, a wide smile, striding his way back home. And as I passed with Nela, I noticed that the embankment covered in bramble on which fennel grew was still there.

But Noiraude the goat had disappeared a long time ago.

We passed Uncle Émile's house. Sold by uninspired heirs (for very little money, I was told) to Parisians who had but a single desire: to remodel the old building to today's standards, inflicting on it a face-lift of sorts to make it look more modern. The façade was sprayed with liquid stucco, then painted orange-red – the colour of blood oranges. The kitchen door and the doors to the upstairs rooms were painted green – parrot green, slightly milky, a little like *pastis* with mint syrup – along with the windows. Green being the complementary colour to red, the whole house cried out for attention from afar. Disappointing!

Further down, the stable had been turned into an apartment, quite comfortable I'm sure, with an entrance that gave directly onto the garden where the linden tree grew. *Pécaïré!* Our old friend was in a sad state indeed. How could he still feel comfortable in his bark living in a time that was no longer his? Though it was late spring, there was no sign on the ground of the sweet-smelling flowers of old. What good would a nap be in the shade of an anaemic tree that offers only a faded perfume? Was it still watered, like Gérard and I used to do, twice a day, with cool, clear water from the Clérissy fountain? Or did it receive only the water from downpours and, in the manner of the Brassens' great oak, was our linden tree sprayed with the urine of dogs come to lift a leg against it?

I'd forgotten the heart that Gé had engraved in the wood! Hidden from prying eyes, a metre from the ground, on the side where the trunk is only thirty centimetres from the terrace's retaining wall. A heart with an arrow through it: "G loves D." The naïve symbol of an illusory future.

Even the quaint name of Caterwaul Lane had disappeared. That backwards part of the village now had an arrogant faience plaque, pompously claiming a new title: "Old Kiln Quarter." Need I say more? The page has been turned, *vaï!*

☙ THIRTY ❧

Antoine brought us into his workshop.

"In Moustiers, you make faience and not porcelain?"

"We don't make, have never made and, hopefully, will never make anything other than faience. Porcelain is an industry; faience is for artists."

He took a plate and broke it on the edge of a table.

"Look, Nela, the red earth inside it: our earth! Black dirt that's fertile, that produces what's called 'yields,' where farmlands and pastures grow – we have none of that here. Our earth is poor. But it's fine too, warm in tone and soft to the touch."

He put a humid lump in Nela's hand.

"Feel the smoothness: a real caress! That is our Provençal earth – earth for artists. With it, everything becomes easy. Remember, Dodo, you take it, you knead like this, you shape it. Then you cook it: 1,020 degrees Celsius. Here, in this oven."

"You don't use the old one anymore?"

"No, these days they're all electric and a hundred times easier to adjust. The secret of all great ceramics is the way the piece is cooked. The solidity of the piece depends on that."

He took a fragment.

"It's very hard. Break this piece."

"I see what you mean."

"Then – you know this, Dodo – you deburr the piece, you touch it up, you play with it until you get what you want. Then it's time to temper it in semi-liquid raw enamel. There, in that tub. Personally, I use only the traditional process, applying the motif with the *grand feu* technique on raw enamel. A secret Pierre Clérissy learned from a monk in Faenza. Then comes the most delicate part of the operation: the decorations. Your work has to be perfect, because it's impossible to touch it up if you make a mistake."

"And what do you do when you mess up?"

"Look, over there, that big garbage can. Just toss it in!"

He put his words into action. A long shot through the air… basket! He obviously wasn't short on practice, old Toinou!

"So the pieces you don't mess up are done?"

"*Daïsé,* Nela, not so quick! Once they're decorated, they're cooked a second time: nine hundred degrees Celsius, to fix the colours and whiten the enamel. You remember, Dodo, when my father and grandfather let us in here? We circled them like flies until they let us show what we were able to do."

"All I remember is that I wasn't very good at it!"

"Gérard was good, especially for the motifs. Would you like to try, Nela?"

"Why not?"

"All right. Take a piece of clay here, right, and roll it in your hands until you get the shape of an olive. Then crush it with your thumb, like so. Show me. Good. You now have a flower's corolla. Then sculpt it with this knife: the petals, the pistil, the stamen…"

"Hum. Like this?"

"Exactly, trim a bit off here. Good. Now make us a stem: five centimetres long, no more. No, slimmer. Good. Attach it to the corolla."

"Okay. And what if I bend the stem a little?"

"Good idea. It'll be prettier still."

Meanwhile, the oven's heat indicator rose. It would be almost ready for the first cooking by the time Nela finished the colours.

"Okay, follow my lead here. Yellow first. Good. Now, with the edge of the knife, draw the petal's veins."

And there was Nela's bouquet: cornflowers, peonies, and buttercups, all with brilliant corollas. Twelve knife-holders that would be cooked in the *"grand feu"* style, in scarcely more time that the Courbons, bakers from father to son, would need to make their anchovy *fougasse*.

Our visit to Moustiers would last only two days. Two days during which we visited every corner of the village, crisscrossing the streets looking for long-lost friends always happy to see me certainly, but their words quickly turned to bitter reflections. Two days spent in a dizzying search for things that no longer were. Soon it was time to leave. Soon the tourists would arrive, and just the idea of being stuck among the hordes of mass tourism made me shudder. I was impatient to quickly put distance between myself and this unspeakably sad present.

We left the land of my childhood through wide doors open to the sky – the Verdon gorges! A few kilometres higher and we reached the hilltop village of Aiguines. Barely noon and time to eat. We stopped at the Altitude 823 Restaurant long enough for scrambled eggs with truffles and a pan of *sanguins*, those delicious brick-red mushrooms that grow at the foot of pine trees. A long look over the Sainte-Croix Lake, dotted with tall multicoloured sails… An instant of happiness in which all but the tranquil scene and rich flavours had lost its importance.

Then, back on the road. We climbed a few kilometres and left the forest that surrounded the village behind, then came upon the ramparts of the Verdon. Nela was eager to see the Emerald Valley that I'd spoken of so highly since our arrival in France. A real mountain road, full of twists and hairpin turns, three hundred metres above a torrent swirling in its narrow bed. The road forced us to slow down and imposed a slow contemplation of the landscape, which pleased my navigator. "Stop, Dominique!" She would have taken a picture at every new vista – the Sublime Cornice, the Cavaliers' Cliff, the Mescla Balcony… Blown away, mouth agape, Nela fell silent. Anything you could say about the imposing cliffs and vertiginous peaks would be inferior to reality.

The road led us to the medieval village of Trigance, from which we would quickly descend all the way to the coast.

❧ THE CURTAIN FALLS ❧

A wonderful start to the evening: twenty-three degrees at six o'clock. In Toronto, autumn is a season of colours. The leaves on our trees are beginning to redden, and soon enough they'll lose them in a blaze of ochre and brown, scarlet and red. Except, of course, for our beautiful blue fir that will resist the cold and snow all winter long.

We would have our aperitif on the terrace and our meal in the dining room, with the door to our yard open, of course.

On the table covered with a white Portuguese tablecloth, each faience flower is set above and to the right of the plate, lined up with the three glasses.

A simple meal, truly Provençal. As an hors d'oeuvre, we'd have toasted bread with *tapenado* on them (an easy recipe: crush black olives, capers, anchovies, a clove of garlic, pepper to taste and a drop of olive oil – then add half a glass of booze "to make the olives sing," as Eugène would say) and a few other spreads, wild boar pâté perfumed with juniper berries (easier still; just open the can). As the main course, a magnificent *pistou* soup! Followed by a cheese plate (goat and ewe, mostly) and a *mesclun* of various greens (the vinaigrette: olive oil, wine vinegar, a hint of garlic – and two or three basil leaves, yes, absolutely!). Then, to finish, the *toucinho de céu* and a profusion of *oreillettes* (Nela's magnificent interpretation, once again, following Henriette's recipe, though calling them *filhós)*, not forgetting a few California figs and other chilled fruits. And, of course, coffee, tea or herb tea (linden). Not to mention the fruit brandies.

Nela would start making the *oreillettes* around six-thirty (the dough had been waiting since our return from *Nova Era*), and I would begin the *tapenado* and the vinaigrette around seven. (She would have finished the *oreillettes* then; best not to be in the kitchen at the same time). Our guests wouldn't arrive until seven-thirty, "French time." I would heat the soup up then – gently: "*Pistou* butter must never cook!" Virginie would say.

★

The cycle of my French *pistou* soups would last more than half a century: from the summer of 1943 to the autumn of 1998 – from the very first that my mother made us in Moustiers out of nothing at all until the last one she made us in Marseille, as per Gérard's request.

In between, death had been at work in our family. Roger was the first to go, killed at the wheel of his Berliet after hitting a sheet of ice and sliding into a plane tree. Then it was

Aunt Marie's turn; she had heart trouble. Followed six years later by her mother, Grandma Rose, whose life ended in bitter despair. My father died in the early 1980s. The following decade, everyone went: Uncle Émile, his son Jean, Uncle Eugène, Félix, Aunt Henriette, then Aunt Virginie, stricken like her mother by the loss of her child. All gone in the space of seven years.

Under this avalanche of bereavement, my mother, then an octogenarian, was like the walking dead. In other words, she fell into deep depression, and her talent in the kitchen suffered too. Her autumn 1998 *pistou*, prepared on the occasion of one of my many trips to Marseille, was completely ruined. Not paying attention properly, my poor mother had bought the wrong variety of basil. And her soup was thin and not smooth at all. The noodles weren't cooked enough, the potatoes had been forgotten and so had the ham. A real catastrophe! Perhaps, subconsciously, she no longer wanted to pit her cooking skills against her dead sister Virginie's. I'll always remember Gérard's face and the look he threw me behind his aunt's back. On his face I could read criticism, resignation, and much compassion for her shipwrecked soul. He bravely let himself be served again and, he – ordinarily so picky – ate his second bowlful down to the last spoonful without flinching. And to think it would be his last *pistou*. Now there is no one left in Marseille to turn the pestle in the mortar...

For Gérard, the consecutive deaths of his father, brother, and mother were like thrusts of a knife of pain that entered each time more deeply. He had never married, and now he felt like a shipwrecked man on a deserted island. Without warning, he had to face himself, convinced that there would no longer be anything interesting in life. Through his open wounds, an immense lassitude and incurable *taedium vitae* poured into him. When, at my initiative, we would conjure up our childhood memories – stockings that didn't owe their silk to the mulberry tree, trains of which he was the great conductor, our epic gastropod hunts – he was barely able to smile. I would say to him, "When you're better…" But he let himself be taken by the first sickness that came along, on the eve of the new millennium that he obstinately refused to enter. And that my mother, already in her ninth decade, would be the first to leave, six years after her nephew.

Now, in Toronto, my *pistou* soups are no longer what they used to be. Exotic with their Provençal accent (no, Gé, I'm not exaggerating), they represent my personal and occasional contribution to meals with my Canadian friends. Typical Canadians, meaning that their origins are diverse enough that, if ever there's another Flood, they could fill out the crew of a new ark that this time would be charged with saving the human race.

At the end of the evening, once the guests have left, I help Nela do the dishes. And if, as I'm drying our beautiful tureen from Moustiers, the good genie we are all waiting for would appear and offer me three wishes, the first that would come to mind would be, my time come – *in hora* – to find myself at a long table on a sea of clouds next to my cousin Gérard. Then, following the order that they themselves have chosen, my beloved Mireille next to Grandma Rose, my Popaul and my Roger shoulder to shoulder, and Aunt Henriette and Nela (who would be discussing *filhós* and *oreillettes*), Aunt Marie and Uncle Émile, and Félix, Jean and Lili, my other cousins.

Then, Virginie would arrive, tureen in hand, escorted by her faithful Eugène. And everyone would applaud long and hard around that joyous table, while a few available leaves would wait in a corner for future generations.

"And Virginie's soup, Eugène, how would it be?"

"The most fragrant, the most satiny, the smoothest, the tastiest of any *pistou*!"

Aunt Virginie's Recipe

Soup au Pistou

For six to eight people

Ingredients:

For the soup:
2 yellow onions
6 potatoes
4 zucchini
1 small leek
300 grams dried beans (red and white)

The pistou "butter":
6 garlic cloves
6 ripe tomatoes
2 cups fresh basil leaves
300 grams grated cheese (parmesan, gruyere, and red dry Edam, 100 grams each)

For the combination:
500 grams pasta (tortiglioni or penne rigate)
200 grams snow peas
1 slice of ham without the skin (San Daniele)

olive oil
sea salt
pepper

Preparation:

1. The Soup

In a heavy kettle, sauté the onion in two spoonfuls of olive oil. Then pour in 2 litres of salted water. Bring to boiling and add the vegetables, except for the peas and the tomatoes. Boil vigorously. After cooking 45 minutes, remove the beans and blend the mixture.

2. The *Pistou* Butter

In a mortar, begin by crushing the garlic, tomatoes and basil leaves with a good pinch of sea salt. Slowly add 10 mL of olive oil. Then add the grated cheeses, continuing to blend with the pestle until the "butter" is smooth.

3. The Combination

Mix together the soup and the butter while heating. Cook the pasta in the combined ingredients (12 to 15 minutes). Five minutes from the end, add the snow peas. Then, when everything is cooked, add the diced San Daniele ham just to warm it through. Let the *pistou* stand several hours. Reheat before serving.

AFTERWORD

The Provençal Language in Moustiers and Marseille in the 1940s

During the time in which this book takes place, the country-side of Provence was largely bilingual, whereas in Marseille, the Provençal language appeared only through the local variation of French.

In Moustiers, the population, no more than three hundred souls, speaks Provençal as its mother tongue and French as its official language. Learned at school, where Madame Dupuis kindly asks the pupils to leave their "patois" at the door, French takes over at the post office, the police station, and at the doctor's and notary's offices. Though it shows up only sporadically, and according to the individual's looks, you might say, at the butcher's, the baker's, and the grocer's (an Italian), and is very rarely invited to the gossip sessions where women knit on the church square and to the men's sacrosanct games of *boules*, where many a glass is raised.

As for the population of Marseille, the largest city outside of Paris, it has always been one of many colours, and therefore polyglot, as we see in the scene at the Saint-Charles train station. Still, it is made up of mostly Provençal people. Though that is the demographic reality, between the two world wars, the Provençal language lost its status, defeated by a language that was both national and international. That's business for you. But before its retreat, that clever language was able to leave its trace in the singsong accent of Marseille,[11] a type of French that, like Massalia itself, born of the distant couplings of foreign princes, sprang from the mixed northern and southern origins of the language itself.

So, Antoine and his mother, cousin Marcel, cousin Jeanne, Tavé the gamekeeper – all these Moustiers characters use their Provençal at the slightest provocation, whereas Uncle Eugène, Virginie, her sisters, young Dominique's cousins and all the rest of the family speak the particular language of Marseille quite naturally, and use Provençal only occasionally and approximately. Where Madame Audibert says *pécaïré*, Grandma Rose settles for *peuchère*, a Frenchified version of that interjection.

Perfectly bilingual, Uncle Émile, who has made a career for himself as a Marseille harbour fireman, is a special case. Just like Uncle Roger, a native of Toulon, who has known Moustiers forever, thanks to his older sister who married, like Aunt Marie, a pure-blooded son of the soil. Roger's deep knowledge of the place, the customs, and the language of the countryside helps him revive a moribund conversation with the shepherd Pau-Parlo ("of few words") who, "having unlearned to speak because of excessive solitude," settles for a wave of his hand and a smile.

All these *estrangié* words that fill *A Pinch of Time* are easy to understand, thanks to their context. They should not prove indigestible for our gentle readers.

ENDNOTES

[1] Translator's note: The expression *baiser* Fanny means to score no points in a match. The losers of a *pétanque* game who didn't manage to score a point, in the South of France, had to kiss the behind of a female cardboard cutout (sometimes a sculpture or naked buttocks made of clay).

[2] Created by Pierre Laval's government under orders from the German authorities, the CWS (or *Service du travail obligatoire* in French) sent some 650,000 people (including 40,000 women) to Germany to join the prisoners of war, "the 1940 guys" who numbered about a million. It is estimated that some 260,000 people managed to escape the CWS.

[3] The French Militia (called the *Milice*) was a political police force that the Vichy regime created at the end of January 1943, based on the Gestapo. Under the supervision of its founder, Joseph Darnand, also its Secretary-General, it followed Pétain's ideology of forceful repression and was the most patent symbol of collaboration with the invader. After occupation, repression.

[4] On November 7th and 8th, 1942, under the American General George Smith Patton, an Anglo-American force got a foothold in Algeria and Morocco. Operation Torch was a military success that worried the Germans. In the home country, retaliation was immediate: the Huns took over our fields on the 11th – a symbolic date – and began to devour our potatoes. Economic exploitation was a heavy burden for France, which quickly became the primary food source for the Reich. Vichy said nothing. But the Résistance quickly declared its intentions. On November 27th, French sailors off Toulon were surprised at dawn by elite units of the Kriegsmarine, and preferred to scuttle their ships rather than let them fall into enemy hands.

[5] "Comprenne qui voudra," *Au rendez-vous allemand*, Éditions de Minuit, Paris, 1945.

[6] An allusion to French singer-songwriter Georges Brassens' *La Tondue.*

[7] *The Peat Bog Soldiers* (originally in German, *Börgermoorlied*) was written in 1933 by German prisoners at the Börgermoor camp. This penitentiary, one of the first Nazi camps, was situated in the marshy area of Emsland.

[8] In the early stages of the Occupation, following the Vichy government's appeal, more than 300,000 volunteers left France for German soil. Later, in 1942, Pierre Laval devised the Relève, whose goal was to slowly repatriate prisoners of war in exchange for volunteer workers. The ingenious system, based on reciprocity, had not worked as intended.

[9] Albert Camus in the journal *Combat*, October 29, 1944.

[10] Adapted from Mary Caws, *Selected Poems of René Char.* New York: New Directions.

[11] This has led two specialists, Philippe Blanchet and Médéric Gasquet-Cyrus, to comment humorously that "Marseille French might be completely French, but it's completely something else!" (*Le Marseillais de poche*, Paris, Assimil, 2004)